ISTANBUL!

a novella

by Tom Eagan

Tom Eagan
2004

ARAN PRESS
Louisville, Kentucky

For Christopher and Allison
two phenomenally great people
with all my love

PUBLISHER'S NOTE

ISTANBUL! is believed to be Number 45 in the lost or hard to find series TALES OF THE HALL. Other numbers in the series may be published if we can only locate them.

Also in the TALES OF THE HALL series, and obtainable wherever quality books are found:

> FIRE DANCERS OF BALI
> BY LOVE REPOSSESSED
> RUMORS OF JUSTICE
> THE SKULL (available 2005)

The complete Aran Press Catalogue is available at our website.

* * *

A SCHOLARLY NOTE FOR
THE LEGAL SCHOLAR

To the gentle, general reader (if there be any), you need not dally over this Note. Please proceed to the Preface.

This Note is provided as a brief apéritif for scholars who have come to revere the TALES OF THE HALL as a chronicle of American legal history.

Please be advised that the position advanced by Professor Armis that ISTANBUL! is a parable on the tragic consequences of the divorce of Law from Morality is a minority opinion.

It is well-settled that the Law was hacked away from its Biblical foundation in a series of Court decisions in the last half of the 20th Century and well into the 21st Century. There can be no dispute that first an amoral and then an immoral and surrealistic culture followed as generations schooled without a moral compass came to rule.

To read ISTANBUL! as part of this sad history is to do justice to neither ISTANBUL! or the theme of American moral decline. The latter (specifically, the role of the Supreme Court as facilitator of moral decline) is best recounted elsewhere. [Editor's Note:See A"LIVING" CON OR A CONSTITUTION? Number 57 in the TALES OF THE HALL series.]

No, ISTANBUL! is more illustrative of the wisdom of state bars allowing for out of state, and most particularly out of country CLE junkets. In today's world the issue may appear quaint. Yet, this can be an issue, under the proper circumstances.

As with the publication of every re-discovered TALE, there has been controversy as to whether ISTANBUL! should properly be included in the TALES OF THE HALL series. In the past, the editors of Aran Press have told how they came upon the manuscript, which hinted at a rationale for a tale's inclusion. With ISTANBUL!, however, the editors have provided no comment save to say: "Go suck a lemon!"

The scholarly backlash has been swift, harsh and furious. As one scholar put it, to include ISTANBUL! in the TALES series is, to put a mustache on the Mona Lisa. Or in the words of the embittered Professor Bicklestaff, "You fools (i.e. the editors of Aran Press) have plunked down a tutti-fruity ice cream in the middle of steak and potatoes!"

Perhaps, considering the nature of the story told in ISTANBUL!, the editors of Aran Press are justified in not revealing how they acquired the manuscript. But the editors will not waiver from declaring ISTANBUL! an authentic number in the venerable TALES series.

Be it noted, the editors have publicly apologized for their referring to "the besotted, senile Bicklestaff and his bloated brigands who monopolize the best chairs by the fireplace of the Antiquarian Club and in their dotage babble about matters they know nothing of."

Needless to say, the editors also regret the consequent and on-going litigation that has resulted from the intemperate exchanges over the inclusion of ISTANBUL! in the TALES OF THE HALL. The dispute, to be sure, has deeply troubled and saddened the scholarly world.

Still, the editorial board of Aran Press to a man stands behind ISTANBUL! as an authentic TALE OF THE HALL. They cite the ground breaking work of Dr. Todd Bolus, professor of legal detritus, as justification.

Dr. Bolus, as you may recall, recently spent several months locked away in his basement pawing over old phone directories and newspapers. Professor Bolus emerged from his basement with a serious lung ailment but fully satisfied that he had discovered many of the names mentioned in ISTANBUL! in one phone directory or another and a name or two here and there in a moldy newspaper.

On the subject of authorship, Dr. Smythe-Wright-Carter advances the theory that ISTANBUL! was written by a secret government agent. The fruits of Dr. Smythe-Wright-Carter's twenty-five years of research should be available in a forthcoming three page monograph. *

Not to steal Dr. Smythe-Wright-Carter's thunder, Professor Horace Longbone is leading the charge in advancing an alternative theory of authorship. Professor Longbone is convinced that ISTANBUL! was concocted by an attorney of the period, one Thomas "Tony" McAdam. There is some dispute, however, as to whether McAdam actually ever existed. (Dr. Bolus could not find his name in any of the phone books in his basement.) Still, Dr. Longbone points to the Preface where it clearly states that the story comes from McAdam.

Which brings us to: How much factual truth is there in ISTANBUL!? Professor N. Pennywitt assures us that the basic story is essentially true and that it is taken from an actual account of a similar incident which might have occurred in either the 1880's or the 1920's, only it did not occur in Turkey and it did not involve attorneys. (See "Good Wine in Cracked Sacks"**)

With regard to factual basis, it would be remiss on our part not to mention in passing the opinion of a once prominently placed source in the intelligence community, who has remarked: "There is a lot of instant bull in ISTANBUL!"

And the opinion of another highly placed source: "That the author of ISTANBUL! was insane is beyond question. What must be questioned is the sanity of anyone who would take the time to read this drivel."

It was such less than kind comments as these that chilled serious study of ISTANBUL! for decades. It is only recently, with the papers delivered at the TALES OF THE HALL symposium at the University of North Windham this past summer, that scholarly attention is again focusing on ISTANBUL!

No doubt, buckets of ink will flow in search of the definitive answers to the above issues. Till the answers are forthcoming, Aran Press is pleased to make the basic text available for the general public.

> — Dr. Randell Fosdick, IV
> Chair of the ISTANBUL! section
> of the Tales of Hall Symposium,
> University of North Windham,
> on the banks of the Windham.
> summer of 2060

* Dr. Smythe-Wright Carter hopes his discoveries will be released to the world in an upcoming issue of *Lex Philologica.* He is shooting for Vol. 4,001, Note #46, pp. 535-538.

** "Good Wine in Cracked Sacks" by Professor Nicholas Pennywitt may be found among his uncollected papers. Apply to David Larson, the Granville Inn, River City.

ISTANBUL!

PREFACE

*I*t was a dark and stormy day. Several attorneys were crammed into Tony McAdam's office on the fourth floor of the old Nash Building on the east side of 5th Street between Jefferson and Market.

We had spent the day wrapping up a complicated legal matter. We might have wrapped up the complicated legal matter a bit quicker if there had not been so many nifty knick-knacks and curios in McAdam's office to distract us — like the Rubik's Cube, the monkey on a chinning bar and the birthday sparklers.

McAdam's office was not your ordinary legal office. Every square inch was cluttered with one toy or another. McAdam's office was more like a novelty store than a law office.

And pictures! Pictures everywhere. Pictures of people you wouldn't expect to see. Like the giant picture of President Millard Fillmore. A picture of Vladimir Ilyich Ulvanov (Lenin) and pictures of Al Capone, Einstein, Niels Bohr, F.H.C. Crick and J.D. Watson and many others.

There were so many pictures in McAdam's office, you might think you were in a theatrical agent's office instead of the office of one of the brightest attorneys in River City.

On one table was the latest copies of the famed *McAdam Report*. *The McAdam Report* was a compilation of news stories and opinions taken from various publications around the world. Tony McAdam regularly put together *The McAdam Report* and made it available via the internet to anyone interested in reading something beyond what the local media had to offer. In his heart of hearts, McAdam was a reincarnation of Horace Greeley.

If you asked McAdam about *The McAdam Report,* he would bring out a box of back issues and bombard you with topics you probably never thought about.

Like, Abraham Lincoln as a villain. McAdam had all the documentation to prove Lincoln was the worst of presidents, and he would gladly share it with you.

(It was kind of ironic that McAdam was so down on Lincoln, being as young Abe, it is said, once had an office in the very old Nash building inhabited by Tony McAdam. Indeed, Lincoln may even have sat in Tony's squeaky armchair. But that is another story. Ask Richard Nash Senior or Junior for the details.)

Another issue on which McAdam stood out as an independent thinker was smoking. Fearlessly going against the tide of public opinion, McAdam maintained that there was no proof that smoking caused any illness or that second hand smoke harmed anyone. On the contrary, McAdam believed that a room full of smoke was a health enhancer, improving both the lungs and the brain's ability to put two and two together or at least one and one.

McAdam did not take unpopular positions for the hell of it. He was just a life-long seeker of the truth. The truth — no matter how many warts the truth might have, no matter how unpopular the truth may be. In the entire country, McAdam was, no doubt, the most brilliant, articulate nonconformist— not institutionalized.

He was also a scrappy attorney who argued most eloquently whatever side he found himself on. [Editor's Note:

For an account of some of McAdam's spectacular legal victories see *Truth Triumphs,* Number 43 in TALES OF THE HALL; Professor Peachum's "Pour Veritas et Personum Indignum," Juris Secundus Trivis, vol 23.; Contra McAdam, see *The Machinations of McAdam,* Number 28 in TALES OF THE HALL and R. P. Scruggs, *Truth McAdamized.*]

It is necessary to give a thumbnail sketch of McAdam because it was McAdam who told me the story that will shortly unfold. If the credibility of the story is to be questioned, seek out McAdam.

As I was saying, a bunch of us were gathered in McAdam's office. The negotiations had worn us out. An agreement, nonetheless, had been patched together. Our clients, not present, would sign the documents. And closure would be brought to the matter.

From a bottom draw of his over-sized desk, Tony produced a bottle for celebration.

(Now I know Tony McAdam will tell you he never brought out a bottle from anywhere because he does not drink. I'm just telling you how I remember it, and if Tony, the truth seeker, wants to say otherwise, it's okay by me.)

After a few laughs, a few drinks, a few cigars lit . . . (Some of those present might even deny the cigar smoking.) . . . the party of adversaries dissolved into a bunch of old chums sitting around shooting the breeze, recalling war stories from the old days.

Somehow the subject of CLEs came up. "CLE," for the uninitiated, is the acronym for "Continuing Legal Education." CLEs are seminars or lectures that attorneys in the state were required to take each year to maintain their license to practice law.

CLEs can be held anywhere. Often vacations are masked as CLEs as when a CLE is held in Las Vegas, New Orleans, or Sweet Pea, Arkansas.

There was general laughter as one story after another was told.

Then, someone mentioned the Istanbul CLE. All laughter ceased. Dead silence. It was an awkward moment. It was as if the person who mentioned the Istanbul CLE had committed a monumental faux pas.

Now here I should mention that at this time I was an out-of-town attorney. I had not yet moved to River City. When the silence fell on everyone in the room, I sensed they all knew something in common that I did not know. Something no one wanted to talk about.

"So what is it about the Istanbul CLE?" I asked. No one answered.

I think it was John Bauman who quickly changed the subject. He popped up out of his chair and looked out the window and observed how the snow was coming down heavier than earlier and he had better get going.

Everyone else immediately followed Bauman's lead. Recalling how they had families waiting for them, they began searching for their coats and briefcases, and muttering how they'd better get on the road while there was still road to get on.

In less than a minute, after perfunctory handshakes, the room was cleared, and it was just McAdam and me.

I had hung behind because I wanted to hear about the Istanbul CLE. I didn't care about the snow piling up outside. I was an out-of-town attorney, booked into a hotel a block and a half away from McAdam's office. At the hotel, not even a goldfish was awaiting my return; I had no need to rush off.

McAdam also seemed perfectly content to just sit. Perhaps, he realized he had too much to drink to even attempt the drive home over an ice covered road.

"So, what's so special about the Istanbul CLE?" I asked, when the others had left. In my mind, it wasn't the snow, but the mention of the Istanbul CLE, that had sent everyone out the door.

McAdam gazed at me for a long moment, as if gauging if I were worthy of hearing the story. He took a puff on his cigar and another sip from his drink.

More silence as he shifted his focus and appeared to contemplate something across the room or perhaps it was the haze from his cigar smoke in the middle of the room that he was studying.

Finally, he addressed me. "I can see you are a person of pedestrian tastes and a conventional mindset."

"What?" It wasn't what I expected.

"'Reality'" he went on, "is defined for you by the nightly T.V. news and the daily newspaper. They are your gatekeepers. For something to be 'real' for you it must be taken note of by the newspaper or the television.

"Anything outside their purview you are uncomfortable with. You think and speak about what the media focuses your attention on and no more. You are totally unprepared to consider as real anything that the media has not endowed with authenticity."

"I don't think—" I began to protest.

"Precisely!" He rolled on. "The Istanbul CLE would only violate your sense of what is possible. To you it would be a mere taradiddle."

"A taradiddle?" I mumbled.

"A piscatorial prevarication," he explained.

"I piss what, you say?" I was at sea.

"A mare's nest of claptrap." With an expansive wave of his cigar, he explained his explanation.

"A mare's nest of claptrap?!" My frustration was percolating to a boil.

"A gooseberry!" He over-enunciated and appeared dismayed at my inability to comprehend what he was saying. "A fabrication! A fairy tale!" He shouted.

"In short," he concluded in a milder tone, "it would be a waste of your time and mine to relate the Istanbul CLE story to you. You are unequipped to handle anomalies. And the Istanbul CLE story is chock-full of anomalies. "

I was insulted. I was outraged. I couldn't follow half of what he was saying. But it evoked memories of my parents telling me, "You're too young to understand."

He was shutting me out from the adult club of those who knew the story of the Istanbul CLE. Which only made me want to hear it more.

"Hey! I've seen gooseberries in my time!" I protested. "And I can certainly deal with anomalies! I'll have you know I've never met an anomaly I couldn't handle. In fact, it's one of the main reasons I became an attorney — precisely — to deal with anomalies!"

(I made a mental note to myself to find a dictionary first chance I got and look up "anomaly.")

He blew some smoke, pressed an index finger against his pencil-thin mustache and gave it some more thought.

At length, he sighed, "Okay. But only if you promise—"

"Promise!" I said, interrupting.

"—not to interrupt." He finished his sentence.

"Promise!" I cried.

"Especially so," he over-enunciated, "with questions
like 'How can that be?!' "

"I promise! I swear I promise!" I held up my hand
taking an oath on it.

He settled back in his chair, looked up at the ceiling
and after a suitable interval he began the prologue.

PROLOGUE

"*T*he Istanbul CLE story is not an easy story to tell. Like an onion with different layers or a series of Chinese boxes, one box within another, the Istanbul CLE story is not just one simple story, but layers of stories and nuanced subtleties, comparable to a Rembrandt. You have to focus your attention to get to the heart of the matter. And at the heart you might find darkness. Or government secrets and the fate of nations." McAdam whispered the last sentence.

"Government secrets and the fate of nations?!" I wasn't sure I heard him right. I was agog.

"Government secrets and the fate of nations," he repeated. "But more of that later." He waved smoke away and coughed. "Far, far more disturbing — at the heart of the matter is a moral dilemma — you might not want to consider, but once you hear about it, it will be with you the rest of your life." He poured himself another drink and held the bottle suspended in air between us. "Are you sure you want to hear the story of the Istanbul CLE?"

I took the bottle. "Yes. Yes!" I said and filled my glass to the brim. I wasn't quite sure what a "moral dilemma" was. But I was young and could think of nothing I could not face.

"Then let's start with the surface level." He drew in a deep breath and pressed the hair down on his head. "Some years ago, twelve attorneys from River City boarded a plane for Istanbul, Turkey."

"Istanbul, Turkey?" I squinted. Again, I thought perhaps I hadn't heard him correctly.

"Right. Istanbul, Turkey." He paused to allow me to absorb the fact that it was Istanbul, Turkey, we were talking about and not Istanbul, Indiana. [Ed. note: There is no Istanbul, Indiana, that we know of.]

He continued: "The ostensible purpose of the trip was to get CLE credits by attending a day-long lecture at the University of Istanbul on the subject of 'World Government and Parking Tickets.'"

"World Government and Parking Tickets." I was frowning.

"Right." McAdam nodded, and looked from left to right as if to make sure the walls did not have ears. He leaned forward and whispered: "The *real* reason for the trip was an enforced vacation for the twelve attorneys in an exotic spot of the world, which would get them away from the day-to-day grind of their legal practice in River City.

"You see, the twelve attorneys needed the vacation, but they never would have taken a vacation because—" He tapped ash from his cigar. "—They were workaholics."

"They were workaholics," I repeated to assure him and myself that I was up to speed.

"Eh, right, workaholics. . . The legal profession is a fine and noble profession, but like crabgrass, it can take over everything in your life, till you have nothing in your life but your professional life."

I looked around at all the "crabgrass" that had taken over McAdam's life, and sipped my drink.

"A certain judge (initials H.W.)," he said switching

into a conspiratorial tone, "concerned for the health and sanity of his workaholic friends, had ordered them to go on the Istanbul CLE."

"Wait a minute," I raised the hand not holding my drink. "A judge can't order something like that!"

"It was a secret order," he replied, carefully making room for his cigar stub in his overflowing desk ashtray.

"A secret order? What are you talking about?" I studied his face to see if he was being serious. His face was his normal pasty pale, riverboat gambler poker player face.

"There are a lot of secret orders. If you don't know that, you don't know diddly." He lit another cigar. There must not have been enough smoke in the room.

"There was nothing on paper, of course." He paused to blow out the match and spit out a bit of tobacco. "The judge merely let it be known to the attorneys that if they did not get on the plane to Istanbul, he and several other judges, unnamed, would rule against everything these attorneys brought into court."

"Do you know how crazy that sounds?" I couldn't resist interjecting. It made no sense to me, even in my near inebriated state.

He looked at me and put the cap on the bottle. "I guess you really are not interested in hearing about the Istanbul CLE." He stood. "It's time to close up shop."

He put his jacket on and crossed from behind his desk toward the outer office. "Are you coming or do you want to stay in my office overnight?"

"Wait a minute," I said, rising on unsteady legs. "I'm sorry. I really do want to hear the story, it's just that — secret orders?! . . . Forcing attorneys to go to Istanbul, Turkey?!

It's a little hard to swallow." I was on my feet without realizing it, blocking his way out of his office.

"Reality is a little hard to swallow, son." He turned his cigar vertical and slipped around me to his outer office. "You're welcome to stay here if you wish. Personally, I'm getting a little hungry."

"Let me buy you dinner," I offered, and found my coat and briefcase and staggered after him.

Half an hour later, after trudging through a block of snow, we were sitting barefoot in The Dixie Lounge, our shoes and socks hung out to dry by the fake fireplace.

The Dixie Lounge was McAdam's favorite watering hole and a popular lunch spot for many downtown workers.

Normally, the Dixie Lounge only served a lunch menu and in the evening was just a quiet bar, frequented by a handful of regulars. But with the big snow and everyone sort of trapped, the kitchen at the Dixie was still cooking this evening.

We didn't get around to a continuation of the Istanbul CLE story until after the main course — the Mexican Mound for McAdam and a couple of cheeseburgers for me, and several more liquid rounds, (I switched to coffee.); and my multiple apologies for doubting any part of the story, and promising to save all questions till the conclusion.

McAdam made it clear that if I could not comprehend the simple notion of a judicial order making attorneys go to Istanbul for a CLE, I would never be able to grasp the great events to come.

Again, I promised to hold my questions till the end.

Another drink, another cigar, and McAdam resumed with gusto:

"You have to understand, the Judge's order was done

out of concern for the health and sanity of friends. In his opinion, they were losing their minds for lack of a vacation.

"How the judge came on his convictions and the extreme method he used to help his friends is a story in itself.

"Seems the judge had attended some seminar on the necessity of relaxation. Most judges, as you know, are themselves stressed out from overwork.

"Anyway, the judge heard, as if for the first time, that stress kills. And he heard that there is a thing called 'Vacation Deficit Disorder.' Which I gather means if you don't take a vacation now and then you're going to be in big trouble.

"The judge took all this to heart and returned from his seminar to the Hall with a keen eye for picking out those who were suffering from 'Vacation Deficit Disorder.' He was certain he found it in the attorneys he ordered on the Istanbul CLE."

"Why Istanbul, Turkey?" I couldn't resist asking. "Couldn't he have ordered them to go to Disney World?"

He glared at me. And I immediately realized I violated the No-Questions-till-the-End Rule. I began to apologize, but we were interrupted by the waitress asking for our dessert order.

McAdam was immediately distracted by the dessert menu. (McAdam exchanged some friendly banter with the waitress and the owner of the Dixie Lounge, which I omit here.)

By the time we had our first round of dessert in front of us, McAdam had apparently forgotten my interrupting with a question.

"It was a curious coincidence," McAdam continued munching happily on French silk pie and sipping coffee, "but just about the time the judge was back from his seminar on the need for vacations, there was an attorney, Art Chalmers, trying to round up colleagues to sign up for the Istanbul CLE.

"The Istanbul CLE was Chalmers' baby. Chalmers had made all the travel arrangements. And, Chalmers had convinced some weak-minded person at the state bar to allow a full year's CLE credit requirement for one lecture on "World Government and Parking Tickets," to be delivered at the University of Istanbul.

"Chalmers was fixated on getting the Istanbul CLE off the ground. But no one was interested, even though the price for a week in Istanbul, was ridiculously reasonable. He had no takers, till . . .

"One day, Chalmers was standing in the canteen line on the second floor of the Hall. He was touting his Istanbul CLE to two attorneys, Millie Sharp and David Weinstein.

"A county attorney, Bob Bohnert, just happened to be there in the canteen line behind them. Bohnert overheard Chalmers talking about Istanbul.

"Well, as luck would have it, Bohnert had actually been to Istanbul. He joined in the Chalmers, Sharp, Weinstein conversation and began singing the praises of Istanbul.

"And sing Bohnert did! It is said by some that an actual glow came over Bohnert's face, or maybe it was just sunlight reflecting off the row of recently polished vending machines. His words turned golden. Bohnert rose almost to eloquence, completely unbefitting and out of character with the normally prosaic, shy, background-kind-of-guy Bohnert for years led everyone to believe he was.

"And what uncorked Bohnert? What brought him to life? Istanbul! What was Istanbul to him or he to Istanbul?!

"And yet, he sang the praises of Istanbul! How Istanbul was this and Istanbul was that! Best vacation spot in the world! The closest thing to heaven —Istanbul! Most fun he had ever had was in —Istanbul! Happiest time of his life was — in Istanbul! Istanbul! Istanbul! Where God would have placed Adam and Eve if He had only given some thought to it. Istanbul! Istanbul! The most wonderful place on the planet! A place of magic and more magic! Magic! Magic! Magic! Blah-blah-blah.

"I'll tell you what is wonderful and magic — wonderful, magical and *dangerous* — what comes of putting different people next to each other in the canteen line on the second floor of the Hall of Justice.

"Things happen when you randomly mix and match people in a canteen line. Especially, when they get to engaging in idle conservation with others, as people have a tendency to do waiting in the canteen line on the second floor of the Hall. They talk and they listen — to perfect strangers. Or they just overhear things. And sometimes lives are changed. Just from people standing in the canteen line and putting their two cents in with someone else's two cents.

"It was certainly the case when Judge H.W. was in line just behind Bohnert and overheard Bohnert sing the praises of Istanbul and Chalmers pitching his Istanbul CLE.

"A light bulb went on in the judge's head. He put two and two together and immediately decided to order his workaholic attorney friends to sign up for Chalmers' Istanbul CLE. Bohnert's words so affected Judge H.W. that he said he would have joined the party, himself, for some of the magic of old Istanbul, but he had too much work to catch up on."

"Didn't any of the attorneys protest being ordered to

go to Turkey for a week?" I couldn't resist asking.

"Oh sure. The usual excuse was they had court appearances scheduled. Judge H.W. brushed that aside. Told them to get Michaels & Howard to cover. [Ed. note: *See, When You're Out, We're In — For You*: the life and times of Michaels Fred and Howard L, Number 42 in TALES OF THE HALL series. Michaels Fred and Howard L. covered so many cases for other attorneys, they were referred to as the "Cover Men."]

"Now one of the attorneys that signed up for the Istanbul CLE was the afore-mentioned Millie Sharp. Millie Sharp, by the way, isn't her real name. I can't give you her real name for reasons that will be made clear later.

"Millie was a family court attorney. She specialized in representing wronged wives in divorce actions. She was very, very good at skinning alive abusive husbands, and emptying out their bank accounts.

"Well, at the time of our story, Millie had quite a reputation. She was in the first rank of divorce attorneys.

"There was only one problem. Because of a combination of circumstances, which we will get to, Millie was burnt out.

"Millie signed up for the Istanbul CLE, she told me, not only because of the judge's order but because Art Chalmers had been hounding her for weeks to sign up. *And* she realized she needed a vacation.

"When she got on the plane for Istanbul, Millie was at the end of her rope. Deep depression. Which she had been seeing a doctor about, but without much success.

"She got on the plane with so much 'psychological baggage' — her words — if it were quantifiable in pounds, the plane would never have been able to get off the ground.

"I must say, and I say this in the strictest confidence," he leaned forward and almost whispered, "she may have been a pathetic mess when she boarded the plane for Istanbul, but to me she was still one of the most beautiful women in existence. She looked a lot like Greta Garbo and her mind was as sharp as Pericles' mistress. . . And, if that ever gets back to my wife,— I will kill you."

I gulped at his intensity. And I made a mental note to look up Greta Garbo and Pericles' mistress.

McAdam sat back and in a normal tone continued, "Enough preliminaries, let's get to the story as told to me by Millie Sharp."

We ordered more cake —cheesecake this time— and more coffee and he began the story of the Istanbul CLE.

CHAPTER 1

"When terror comes, they will seek peace,
but there will be none."
— Ezekiel 7:25

*A*ll Millie wanted was peace.

She had always wanted peace. As a young girl she marched in all the marches to keep America out of every war. She lit candles and chanted with the crowd, "All we are asking is give peace a chance."

She was for the Peace Corps. She was for Greenpeace. Any organization with "peace" in its name— she sent them a generous contribution.

She was against violence in all forms: against cutting down trees to make houses; against slaughtering animals for food or clothes. (Once she picketed McDonald's and she definitely would never be seen in a fur coat. As an attorney, she had sued to allow sparrows, pigeons and blue jays the right to fly where they wished and defecate at will. She also defended the rights of squirrels not to be shot; fish not to be caught and horses not to be rode.) She was against SUVs, which killed people. She was very much for gun control. No one should be allowed to have any kind of gun, not even a popgun! (Paint guns were okay, but the name should be changed.) Why couldn't everyone be reasonable and just talk out their differences and get along?! Or if they weren't inclined to talk, do yoga or transcendental meditation.

And now more than anything, she craved a personal peace. Tragedy had collapsed Millie's world, and sapped her

will to go on. There was no purpose or joy left. When meditation and herbal tea failed, she reached out and found a doctor who gave her pills. Pills that dulled the pain. But neither
doctor nor pills could restore purpose, joy or peace.

(It wasn't peace, but sometimes she would go into
fits of giggling, which was one of the side-effects from one
of the pills. And sometimes on another pill, she would "zone
out" and not remember where or who she was for a few minutes . . .or days. An unfortunate side-effect of a pill that was
spordatically effective at chasing the blues away.)

Yesterday her doctor gave her a new pill or rather 400
big shinny metallic blue pills; "mega-medicine" he called it.
And he gave her his blessing for her to get on a plane to
Istanbul. "A vacation might just be the ticket, but take one of
the 'big blues' every four hours, too," her doctor advised.

And so she was going to Istanbul. Taking a vacation
from her domestic law practice, where there was never any
peace, only wailing and gnashing of false teeth, recriminations on recriminations, and brain surgery was done with a
meat cleaver.

Perhaps, she wouldn't find the magic that Bob Bohnert
had found in Istanbul, but she hoped in a week's vacation to
maybe find a quaint little shoppe in old Istanbul where she
could purchase a small authentic Turkish carpet.

She was traveling with dear friends: David Weinstein,
John Fowler, Mary Jo Wicker and Art Chalmers. All right,
maybe they weren't really dear friends. Maybe they were
only colleagues she interacted with professionally and never
saw outside professional settings and professional communi-
cations. But they were the closest things to friends that she
had.

For Millie, there was no personal life. It was all work, work, work. Still, she had known her "friends" for years. Like herself, they were all serious, competent, honest, hardworking, no-nonsense attorneys. People she felt comfortable with, even though she knew nothing or very little of their private lives, or if they even had private lives.

And there were some other attorneys on the trip, which she knew by reputation to be serious, competent, honest, hardworking, no-nonsense attorneys — Tom Schwietz and a bunch of attorneys who did almost exclusively criminal law — Larry Simon, Casey McCall, David O'Brien and the great J.R. Moore and his nephew, the silent, humble-appearing Steve Esselman.

And there was one odd ball. One attorney, Robert Render, about whom she knew nothing. Nobody did. Render kept to himself and never exchanged a pleasantry with anyone.

The party departed early Sunday morning from River City on flight 433 to Detroit, where they switched planes to a flight that took them to New York's Kennedy Airport, where they were to catch a transAtlantic flight that after a stop here and there in Europe would get them to Istanbul about fourteen hours after leaving River City.

On the flight from River City to Detroit, David O'Brien provided a surprise. He brought out a dime-store ukulele and began singing and playing — songs like "Buffalo Girls won't you Come out Tonight and Dance By the Light of the Moon."

Esselman, seated across the aisle from O'Brien, got out of his seat and was tap dancing in the aisle to O'Brien's ukulele. Schwietz clapped and sang along and passed a bottle of rye whiskey to one and all — till the stewardess came down the aisle, confiscated the bottle and made everyone sit down and be quiet.

On the flight from Detroit to New York, O'Brien came out with his ukulele again and began playing a medley of Latin favorites —"Malaguania," "La Cucaracha," "Brazil" and "Spanish Eyes." And Esselman danced the mambo, salsa, bolero, cha-cha and tango in the aisle with a very attractive young lady from Puerto Rico.

Schwietz sang along, clapped hands to the music and passed a bottle of Chianti in a paper bag up and down the aisle —till the stewardess came down the aisle, took the bottle of Chianti and made everyone sit down and be quiet.

All in all, it was a pleasant trip from River City to New York. In New York, they ran into a problem:

The airline they were booked on to make the last leg of the journey filed for bankruptcy over the weekend, and canceled the flight that would have taken them via Europe to Istanbul.

The River City party found themselves stranded at Kennedy Airport, sitting in "the lost passengers waiting area" while Art Chalmers was running around trying to find an air-line that would honor their reservations.

It was while sitting in the lost passengers waiting area, amidst a sea of refugees from all over the world, that Millie experienced sensory overload. There was just too much go-ing on around her. Too many families. Too many bare-breasted mothers suckling babies. Too many children run-ning wild. Too many people munching on saltines. One old man was feasting out of a garbage can. Too many oddly dressed people. Too much loud music. Too many strange tongues.

Millie drew into herself, away from the noises, disturbing images and discussions. She began to wonder if going to a strange land was going to bring peace.

She surveyed her own group, which was pretty quiescent compared to the surrounding sea of humanity. Weinstein appeared to be sleeping; Fowler and Mary Jo were debating which was more intelligent: French bulldogs or Serengeti zebras.

O'Brien was sipping something from a pocket flask and entertaining a group of refugee kids with his ukulele. Playing songs like "Coming to America" and "Greensleeves." The kids were mesmerized; they either had never seen or heard a ukulele before or they had never seen or heard an O'Brien before.

Schwietz was over by the windows, pointing at planes taking off and landing. Casey McCall was reading a big fat book. Larry Simon was working on a legal brief he had been working on since they left River City. His papers and files were spread over several seats. J. R. Moore was working on a crossword puzzle he began when they left River City. Esselman was talking on his cell phone. Render, the only one in a suit and tie, was seated as still as a deserted store manikin. He had a mysterious little box in his lap. Some refugee children were staring at him, but he ignored them.

A thought came into Millie's head. It drifted in like a feather. It was the notion that one of her group, one of her "friends" was in on a plot to kill her. She smiled at the thought. What a silly thought.

Chalmers returned.

"I've got us a plane, but some of you might not like it," he told the group.

He was right there.

The only airline he found that would honor their tickets from the bankrupt airline, and get them to Istanbul *on time* was a new startup Arabic airline, Le Fatalé. If they rushed down to Gate 2001, there was an Le Fatalé flight about to take off. It would get them to Istanbul on schedule, after a few pit stops in various African countries.

They couldn't sit in the lost passengers waiting area forever. What was the alternative? Return to River City? Or pay for a flight on a functioning airline with no guarantee they could get a flight that would take them all and get them to Istanbul on schedule.

Reluctantly, they went down to Gate 2001. And there was Le Fatalé's "Flight Number One." They viewed the plane through the boarding area's bay window. It didn't look like any other plane Millie had ever seen. Except maybe in an old black and white movie; she couldn't recall which movie it was.

"I'm not getting on that!" Weinstein voiced the opinion of almost all.

Almost all. Art Chalmers, who had invested so much time in putting the Istanbul CLE together, urged the group on to the plane. He reminded them of all the magic Bohnert spoke of, and of the Ottoman Grande, the five star hotel with a world class chef they would be staying at.

Larry Simon said the plane had to be safe because FFA regulations required that it be safe and the FFA wouldn't let an unsafe plane enter American airspace.

Tom Schwietz, who had been an Air Force pilot for ages, before he was an attorney, appeared to delight in getting on strange planes. He assured everyone everything would be okay and was the first to board.

Reluctantly, the rest of the group followed. "What the hell, wake me when we land in Istanbul," said Weinstein and followed the others onto the plane.

"At worst," Schwietz said to no one in particular when they were all seated in the plane, "It'll be an adventure." He was as happy as a ten year old who talked his parents into getting on a rollercoaster.

Most of the "parents" agreed with Weinstein—they would snooze across the Atlantic.

But Millie wouldn't sleep. She would observe her "friends" closely looking for signs of which one was in on a plot to kill her. It might seem like an utterly ridiculous idea, but what if it were her intuition alerting her. Millie always relied on her intuition. Intuition was the foundation of her domestic law practice, and her intuition was never wrong.

There was a bit of a stir when the plane took off and they heard not the hum of jet engines, but the whop-whop-whop of propellers. They hadn't noticed that Le Fatalé's Flight Number One was a propeller plane. One propeller under each wing.

The plane got off the ground without incident and after a couple of circles found its bearings, and headed straight east across the Atlantic.

When everyone was settled down and the whop-whop-whop of propellers was just background noise, O'Brien brought out his ukulele and began softly playing Gershwin and Porter classics — "I've Got Rhythm," "Dancing in the

Dark," "Easy to Love," music suitable for the dinner hour.

(There were no actual dinners served on Le Fatalé's Flight Number One, only packets of saltine crackers.)

Soon Esselman was out of his seat ballroom dancing cheek to cheek up and down the aisle with Flight Number One's one and only stewardess.

Schwietz was not singing or clapping his hands to the music this time. He was too busy studying the structure of the plane and sipping from a private flask.

There was general applause as Esselman took a final bow, fell into the seat beside J. R. Moore, and shortly there after fell asleep with a smile on his face.

J. R. Moore hadn't participated in any of the singing or dancing. In fact it is said J.R. hadn't sung, danced or drank since he was in the sixth grade, when with a papier-mâché head he played a donkey in a Doctor Doolittle play.

Now, many years later, J. R. was absorbed in a crossword puzzle he had been working on for over ten hours. Aside from an occasional, "Sit down, you're making a fool of yourself," he pretended to ignore the antics of his nephew. With tight lips, he absorbed himself in his puzzle.

J.R. was one the sharpest wits in the Hall, but he always maintained the dignity of an attorney. One might catch him on an off-day, while playing golf or traveling to Istanbul, in a plaid shirt and short pants, but by gad, no one would ever catch J.R. singing or dancing! Never! Never again, after getting a bad review for his 6th grade performance as a donkey from a little girl with golden locks who accused him of being a sissy.

Behind J. R. and Esselman, sat Larry Simon, busy as a squirrel, scribbling away on his legal brief. Millie stared at

him. A plane ride with no inflight movie gave her the opportunity to stare and wonder if any of her friends were in on a
plot to kill her. It struck her, with his retreating hairline and
glasses, how much Larry looked like Walt Disney's Geppeto,
the tailor who made Pinocchio out of a block of wood. Why
had she never seen the resemblance before? And, the next
moment, (as he fastidiously selected saltine crackers from
the tray of packets of saltine crackers proferred by the stewardess) — how much he reminded Millie of the movie actor,
Dustin Hoffman.

Two seats behind Simon sat Casey McCall, still reading his big fat book.

Directly behind Simon, in front of McCall and across
the aisle from Millie and Chalmers, David Weinstein slouched
in his seat with a smile on his face and his hands folded over
his stomach. The smile on his face said everything. No calls.
No court appearances. Just rest. Nothing was needed to en-
tertain him. He would remain in that position if permitted for
the week. He had been like this for the last ten hours. They
only knew he was alive when they had to switch planes.

John Fowler and Mary Jo Wicker sat in the seats directly in front of Millie. They were debating, from what Millie
could hear, which was more intelligent: a shetland pony or an
Afghan hound. Fowler's passion was dogs; Mary's horses.
The debate raged on.

In the seat directly behind Millie, Robert Render was
straightening his tie. He was always straightening his tie, as
if he were trying to hang himself. It was said by some that
Render was a genius and by others that he was evil. Now
there's a nice combination! He couldn't be in on the plot to
kill her, that would be too obvious. Though Millie wanted to

ask him: Did he realize he looked like a young Bela Lugosi?

Beside Millie sat Art Chalmers. Dear Art was babbling about the history of Istanbul, going back three thousand years before Christ. And every once in a while, he would remind her for the umpteenth time of the five star hotel, The Ottoman Grande, they would be staying at — the best hotel in Istanbul and how it served the best cuisine on two continents.

Among all the things to see and do in Turkey, he told her, he especially looked forward to driving down to the ruins of Troy or as he referred to it, the "cradle of Western civilization."

Chalmers was like a travelog. It was all too much to comprehend at one sitting, even in ten hours of sitting. Millie smiled politely and nodded, as if intently listening. In her head she was absorbed in her own question: Which one of these attorney friends was involved in a plot to kill her?

Millie tried to stay awake to observe her friends, but she dozed off. Maybe it was carbon monoxide seeping into the passenger compartment or the rarified air of the altitude they were flying at creeping into a less than perfectly pressurized cabin or maybe it was just that she was tired. To the loud drone of the propellers and the drone of Art Chalmer's voice beside her recounting the eleven centuries the Byzantine Empire held sway in the world, Millie fell into the land of Nod somewhere over the Atlantic.

* * *

She was rudely awakened by Chalmer's shaking her shoulder and shouting "Millie, wake up! We're going down! If we're going to die, you might want to be awake for it!"

Chalmer's was shouting over a loud high pitched

sound like a hundred washing machines gone berserk. There was the taste and smell of something burning.

Millie opened her eyes to everyone out of their seats and in a general panic. Black smoke covered the left wing and there was no whop-whop-whop from the propeller on the left side of the plane. Only the high pitch whine of a hundred broken washing machines and a 45 degree tilt to the left.

It was all going on at once — Esselman was up doing a modern dance as O'Brien accompanied him on his dime store ukulele. It sounded like "There's Got to Be a Morning After" followed by the "High and the Mighty."

J. R. was on his knees in a prayer circle with some Arabs. "Please God!" he was crying, "I'll sell my golf clubs! No more egg sausages on biscuits in the morning! I'll go back to bananas! I'll never wear another quality suit! Everything I earn will go to whatever church you want, just let me get out of this in one piece!" The Arabs were appealing to Allah in their own language.

Larry Simon's eyes were wide open over his spectacles. "This isn't right! Something is definitely wrong! Someone must *tell* someone! The FFA, the NTSB must be notified! FEMA, the EPA, the WTO — Definitely CBS, ABC and NBC, maybe NABISCO! *Someone* must be informed as to what is happening here!" He was frantically pushing buttons on his cell phone, and crying into it, "Hello? Anyone there?!"

Weinstein was holding hands with the stewardess. They were talking to each other in a language Millie didn't recognize. She was surprised Weinstein was able to communicate in the stewardess's language.

Art was reading from a copy of the *Iliad*.

Casey stood glassy-eyed, mesmerized by the smoke on the left wing. He tossed his book and surveyed those around him as if to say, I'm going to have to die with *these* people? Smoke was beginning to fill the passenger compartment. Maybe he was right.

Millie turned to see Render had not left his seat but was straightening his tie. For a second, he reminded Millie of Herman Melville's unflappable Bartleby, the Scrivener. Was he aware the plane was going down?! Should she tell him?

"I've got the stick here, folks!" came Tom Schwietz's voice over the intercom. "Everyone keep your breeches on!"

No one was listening. In the seats directly in front of her, Millie heard John Fowler and Mary Jo Wicker discussing who would be suing whom as a result of the the plane ditching in the Atlantic; in what jurisdictions the complaint could be filed; who should be named as defendants and what would be a fair settlement.

Suddenly, Weinstein shouted at the stewardess, "You're telling me there are no life preservers on a plane flying across the Atlantic?!"

"Everyone please grab a seat!" Schwietz's voice came again over the intercom. "Everything will be a-okay!" He sounded like a happy carnival barker. Millie wondered if dying was his idea of fun.

A moment later, the unbelievable happened. The plane sort of leveled out, the high pitch whine stopped and somehow the plane seemed to warble along with an oscillating tilt to the left.

In response, everyone with heavy breathing returned

to their seat and sat motionless. Twenty minutes later, Schwietz's voice announced over the intercom, "Don't anyone sneeze. Keep your fingers crossed. If we're lucky, we're going to make an unscheduled landing . . .somewhere."

And they did! The plane landed at Casablanca and everyone got off on wobbly knees.

Tom Schwietz was the hero who brought the plane in. He was surrounded by the press, airport authorities and everyone who wanted to hear all the details. The experience seemed to have rejuvenated him. He began telling the reporters about other planes he had brought in on a wing and a prayer, and made it sound like an everyday occurrence for him in the days before he settled down to being a River City attorney.

"First Junker 88 I ever brought in," he admitted. He went on to tell his audience that the smoking rubble on the runway was a refurbished, disguised, but genuine, bona fide Junker bomber, used by the Nazis in the Battle of Britain in 1940.

There was a stunned silence. Without anyone actually saying it, there was the general sense that it was a madman who just landed the plane safely.

Immediately, the reporters and authorities began wondering where the real pilots were. What was their version of events? Apparently, the pilots were too sick to fly the plane and not up to giving any statements, and nowhere to be found. Nor was any spokesman for Le Fatalé available.

The River City party had mixed feelings about Schwietz. They were grateful to him for saving their lives; but they were angry with him for talking them into getting on the damn plane in New York.

There was debate among the attorneys of catching the next flight back to New York. Almost everyone voted to return to America. Art Chalmers urged them onward. "Istanbul is only a couple of hours away!"

Larry Simon wondered aloud if they returned without having attended the CLE would they be in contempt of Judge H.W.'s order. Everyone looked at Larry with contempt.

"He's not as myopic as you, Larry! We'll explain it to him [Judge H. W.] and arrange to go somewhere else, like we should have in the beginning!" J.R. said. "Like Florida!"

Again, as almost in a replay of their dilemma in New York, the general consensus was to return to River City. Any combination of planes they might catch that would get them back to the USA, however, wouldn't get them there for a week and a half, which meant they would be late in returning home. Which meant they would miss court appearances. This was unthinkable to workaholics. Vacation was one thing, but not being back in court *on time,* was irresponsible and simply unacceptable.

The next plane to Istanbul was right there for the taking. It would have them in Istanbul in three hours. It was not a World War II relic, but a sturdy Boeing 727, the workhorse of international flights.

Again as at Kennedy Airport, Chalmer's recited all the pleasures of ancient Constantinople/Istanbul that awaited them. He reminded them again, they had reservations at the Ottoman Grande, a five star hotel with a world class chef. One day of a lecture and the rest of the time till Friday was theirs to enjoy! Bohnert's endorsement of Istanbul was invoked: best time he had ever had, a wonderful vacation spot; a place of magic.

And so, going with the flow, they boarded the Boeing 727, which was a first class flight, with no one else going their way but a few tired businessmen. They seemed to almost have the plane to themselves.

They were surprised to find Schwietz already aboard. He was smoking a cigar and recounting to an attractive stewardess sitting on his lap how he had brought the Junker in and how, if need be, he could just as easily bring in the 727. The stewardess, bubbling with admiration, was refilling his glass with complimentary champagne.

The trip was three pleasant hours.

John Fowler and Mary Jo were back to debating which animals were smarter. The debate had shifted to which was more intelligent: the Tennessee Walking horse or the Irish setter.

O'Brien warmed up his dime store ukulele with a smooth rendition of the "William Tell Overture," and then accompanied Esselman's "Swan Lake" interpretative dance.

Esselman's dancing was truly amazing. In the Hall Esselman moved like a stooped shouldered zombie, a creature from Chaplin's *Modern Times* or Werner Hertzog's *City of Lights*. But here in the aisle of the 727, it was magic time! Here Esselman came to life. More than life —He danced as gracefully as a string puppet. Which in many ways he resembled — a string puppet: large dark eyes that appeared to be painted on, over-sized facial features. His head, about a foot in front of his shoulders, seemed to move independently of an almost non-existing torso. Arms and legs floated in air and his hands had a life of their own. His performance was beauty in motion.

J.R. ignored his nephew and was back to working his crossword puzzle.

Simon was back to working on his legal brief.

McCall was back to reading his big fat book.

Chalmers and Weinstein were exchanging jokes on computers.

Render was, as always, just there.

And Millie was back to sitting very still and listening to what her intuition might say. Only her intuition wasn't saying anything. Perhaps, her subconscious was sleeping.

Gradually, after another one of the big blue pills, Millie began to look on the bright side. She began to think of all the wonderful things she could see in Istanbul, and of the Turkish carpet she would bring home and put beside her bed. She fancied herself sitting on her authentic Turkish carpet and closing her eyes and in her imagination flying anywhere in time and space.

She watched Esselman pirouette down the aisle to the rhythm of O'Brien's dime store ukulele.

Perhaps, this was the turning point. Perhaps, life was good after all. Perhaps, a week in Istanbul would be a great and wonderful week. Certainly all of the danger of getting here was behind them, and the idea that some one was in a plot to kill her was just silly nonsense.

The plane banked over the ancient, enchanted city that sat on two continents. "Ladies and gentlemen, please take your seats, we will be landing in minutes."

Yes, Millie told herself as the plane touched down in Istanbul, everything was going to be okay.

Then Esselman got shot.

CHAPTER 2

"The matter is too big for any mortal man
who thinks he can judge it."
— Aeschylus
The Eumenides

*W*hen Esselman was shot, he was talking on his cell phone. Standing, talking on his cell phone was Esselman's basic activity in life every day in the Hall of Justice.

When he got shot, however, he was not in the Hall of Justice. (No sheriff in the Hall would have allowed him to get shot.) No, when he got shot, he was in the customs line at Atatürk International Airport, Istanbul, Turkey.

It was just about one a.m., Monday morning. There were only fifteen people left in the customs line — three tired Turkish businessmen and twelve tired attorneys from the U.S.A.

The shooter came out of nowhere, shouted something, fired one round and disappeared into nowhere. It all happened in less than a second.

Millie was directly in front of Esselman. She was having a heated discussion with the customs agents over her pills. Somehow, the customs agents were of a mind that it would not be good for Turkey if she were allowed to enter the country with these giant blue pills.

Weinstein was attempting to assist Millie by speaking to the customs agents in their own tongue. The customs agents appeared not to be convinced by whatever Weinstein was saying to them.

And then came the shout of something by someone and the popping sound of the gun, and Esselman slid to the floor, his cell phone sailing into the air, and all debate over pills was suspended.

The customs agents immediately joined Esselman on the floor. And so did everyone else. Except Millie; she remained standing.

She turned and saw J. R. catching Esselman's cell phone as it sailed through the air. Someone on the cell phone was yelling, "Yo, Esselman!"

Lying on the floor, J. R. carried on a conversation on Esselman's cell phone while checking to see if Esselman was still breathing.

Mary Jo was shaking Esselman "Steve! Steve! Steve!" As if shaking and name calling were cures.

A whistle blew from somewhere and in the next instant, everyone on the floor was surrounded by men in green uniforms, black boots and toting machine guns.

The soldiers with jerking motions pointed their guns in every direction it was physically possible to point a gun. Their eyes darted here, there and everywhere. Were they trying to shoot a lawless fly?

Those on the floor had only one focus of attention — the fingers on the triggers of the rapidly moving machine guns.

The dance of the machine guns came to an abrupt end with the arrival of the "officials." All of the soldiers came to attention and saluted.

The short fat official introduced himself and his companion, the tall thin official:

"I am Inspector Mohammed Abdul Mohammed with the Istanbul Police," announced the short fat official. "And this is Special Army Inspector Jurice Kamal.

"Everyone who is alive, please stand up — slowly." Inspector Mohammed Abdul Mohammed gave his first order.

Everyone who was still alive stood up — slowly.

Esselman did not stand up. All eyes focused on him.

"Ah, ha!" exclaimed Inspector Mohammed Abdul Mohammed, as if discovering Esselman not standing up had solved the crime.

"He needs medical attention, right away!" Mary Jo cried and rushed to Esselman's side.

Inspector Mohammed Abdul Mohammed snapped his fingers and soldiers pulled Mary Jo away from Esselman.

"Madam, do not tamper with the evidence. I decide who needs medical attention and when he needs it — if he needs it. — You!" The Inspector's attention shifted to J.R. who was just concluding the conversation on Esselman's cell phone and making entries in his palm pilot. "Give us that!" Again, he snapped his fingers and a soldier took the cell phone and palm pilot from J.R.

"This is outrageous! We are American citizens! That is my property! And that is my nephew," J.R. cried, pointing at Esselman. "You are treating us as if we were suspects!" J.R. must have thought he was back in the Hall arguing a case to a District Court judge.

"I advise you to hold your mouth shut till questions are asked of you, sir. Or you will be charged with interfering with official police business. Interfering with official police business in Turkey carries a twenty year sentence." Inspector Mohammed Abdul Mohammed paused to see if J. R. had anything else to say.

J.R. tightened his lips and slanted his head to one side. His body language seemed to convey the message, Our turn will come.

"Does anyone else have anything to say?" Inspector Mohammed Abdul Mohammed challenged.

"We have a right to speak to the American Ambassador!" said Schwietz.

Inspector Mohammed Abdul Mohammed eyed Schwietz up and down. "Yes, you have that right, and you can wait in a jail cell till your Ambassador arrives from Ankara. Which may be in two months. I understand he is still on vacation."

There was silence. Inspector Mohammed Abdul Mohammed had won. "Now, one by one I want to hear from each of you what happened."

And so each of the Americans, the three Turkish businessmen and the two customs agents were taken at a distance from the others for an interview by Inspector Mohammed Abdul Mohammed, the fat one, and Special Army Inspector Jurice Kamal, the thin one.

The thin one said nothing. The fat one asked all the questions. The thin one, Special Army Inspector Jurice Kamal, just stood by listening and tapping his riding crop in the palm of his left hand. Yes, he had a riding crop and wore polished black boots and a freshly pressed uniform that looked a lot like a World War I British officer's uniform. He had a cold stare that bordered on the fanatical. The demeanor of the thin Inspector was much more terrifying than the words of the fat Inspector.

The questioning took about two hours and was very thorough. The interviewees were required to empty out their pockets and take off their shoes, and were patted down for anything suspicious they might be carrying. All cell phones and palm pilots were confiscated.

All this time Esselman lay on the floor and no one was allowed to touch him. When the Americans started talking among themselves they were told to keep quiet.

When everyone had been questioned, Inspector Mohammed Abdul Mohammed reenacted the shooting. He had everyone stand where they were standing when the shot was fired. Soldiers held Esselman up in place.

What Inspector Mohammed Abdul Mohammed seemed to be most interested in was the trajectory of the bullet. He went to the wall where the bullet might have lodged if it passed through Esselman. "Hm. There appears to be no damage to the airport. This is good."

He turned his attention to Esselman, who was now back on the floor. Without touching Esselman, he walked around him as one might walk around an automobile one was considering purchasing.

Millie was waiting for him to kick the tires on Esselman. Only there were no tires to kick.

Finally, Inspector Mohammed Abdul Mohammed made his decision. He snapped his fingers and gave an order. "Take him." It was that simple.

Two soldiers took up Esselman and began carrying him off.

J.R. started to follow.

"You! Stay here!" commanded Inspector Mohammed Abdul Mohammed.

"He's my nephew!" cried J.R. "I want to be with him."

"He is not your nephew to me! He is evidence!"

"Evidence?" J.R.'s head tilted and his jaw dropped as it often did when a prosecutor was making a point.

"Where are you taking him?" asked Mary Jo.

"Depends." Inspector Mohammed Abdul Mohammed yawned. Clearly, he was up past his bedtime. "That's for later."

"When can we see him?" J. R. asked.

"Call tomorrow afternoon. Late afternoon. We may be able to answer that."

"Can I get the cell phone and palm pilot back then, too?" J. R. asked.

Inspector Mohammed Abdul Mohammed ignored the question and turned his attention to all the detainees:

"I am sorry to have inconvenienced everyone. But as you can see something serious happened here tonight or I should say this morning. I have talked to you all and I have a clearer picture of what happened.

"You two," he addressed the customs officers. "Go home."

The two customs officers ran out of the terminal as quick as bunny rabbits.

The gate where the incident had happened had been shut down. If there were other planes arriving and people leaving or coming, it was not visible to those detained.

"You three." He pointed at the Turkish business men. "I want more answers." He snapped his fingers and soldiers took the business men off. The faces of the businessmen registered a stoic resignation.

There was only the Americans left.

The Americans braced themselves for the snap of the fingers and the soldiers leading them off, too, for "more answers."

Instead, they got a surprise. Inspector Mohammed Abdul Mohammed smiled and with not a trace of sarcasm or apparent awareness of the utter irony, he turned into the Welcome Wagon:

"Welcome to Turkey! Welcome to Istanbul! It is unfortunate your arrival coincides with this unfortunate incident. But be assured, we will get to the bottom. We will find the culprit and he will pay for his crime.

"Till then, go! Enjoy! Enjoy all the treasures and pleasures of the greatest metropolis in the world. Enjoy your seminar and enjoy the Ottoman Grande. I recommend the oyster soufflé. Enjoy. Enjoy.

"Take up your luggage and go." With a grand gesture worthy of a quiz show moderator informing contestants of their prizes, he indicated their traveling bags.

Soldiers brought out the traveling bags to the Americans. From the articles of clothing sticking out of the suitcases, it was clear the suitcases had been gone through while they had been interrogated.

The Americans were not going to cavil over the sloppy repackaging. They grabbed their luggage and headed toward the exit.

"There is just one thing. . ." Inspector Mohammed Abdul Mohammed cried to them. The Americans stopped, turned and held their collective breath.

"Do not leave Istanbul — till we get to the bottom of this. There might be more here than meets your eyes. None of you are to leave Istanbul, understand? Till we have apprehended the criminal and he has been brought to justice. Is that clear?"

The Americans nodded assent, and before they could take another step toward the terminal exit, a whistle blew and Inspector Mohammed Abdul Mohammed, Inspector Jurice Kamal, and the contingent of soldiers flew past and out the exit.

Slowly the Americans, who appeared to be the only ones in the terminal, picked up their bags and left.

It was about four a.m. Clouds overhead and a light drizzle and a muggy atmosphere greeted them. There was no one on the road in front of the terminal. No vehicles. No people. Nothing.

"Wasn't there suppose to be someone here to meet us?" O'Brien asked of the great CLE planner, Art Chalmers.

Art did not reply. Normally, smiling and upbeat, he looked depressed.

"That was three hours ago. Maybe when they saw the soldiers they ran off. Wouldn't you?" Mary Jo came to Chalmers' defense.

O'Brien, shrugged and took out a cigarette.

Some more moments passed. "Where the hell are the cabs in this greatest metropolis in the world?" Weinstein wondered aloud.

"Maybe it's great because it shuts down at night," Fowler muttered. "Dogs like quiet nights. People who like dogs would like them too."

A few more moments of silence.

"Let's find a phone and see if we can get a cab here," said McCall. He started looking around for a phone.

"Make it three cabs," Schwietz said.

There was no phone visible. No one made a move. No one said anything.

Moments passed and then suddenly from nowhere an old black VMW van with one headlight came down the road and stopped in front of them. The front window rolled down and a man in a wrinkled white suit shouted out at them, "Americans from River City?"

He introduced himself as Mustafa Mohammed and apologized for being late. "Heavy traffic. Very, very heavy," was his only explanation.

Relieved to see him, the Americans were more than willing to excuse a three hour late arrival. For once things were going right by going wrong.

Mustafa helped them load their suitcases into the van which had the vague smell of fish about it and everyone squeezed in and they sped off into the night.

At first it looked like they were headed toward bright lights that could have been the central area of downtown, but Mustafa veered off, and increasingly they were traveling down narrower, darker streets that needed repair. The route did not suggest the way to any grand hotel.

"Is this a short cut to the Ottoman Grande?" inquired Schwietz.

Mustafa did not respond. He had an earplug in his right ear with a wire running down into his white suit.

Schwietz assumed Mustafa might be a bit deaf. So he asked louder: "Is this a short cut to the Ottoman Grande?"

"Ottoman Grande?!" replied Mustafa. "No. There has been a change of plans."

CHAPTER 3

"It was a terrible, strange-looking hotel."
— *Truman Capote*
Other Voices, Other Rooms

"*You* ou are all very lucky, no?!" said Mustafa when asked about the "change of plans."

"Lucky?!" cried McCall from the back of the van. "Lucky?!" McCall looked like he might reach forward and strangle Mustafa.

"If it had not been for heavy traffic—" (Mustafa paused to spit out some of the black stuff he was chewing.) "—and I arrived on time and taken you to the Ottoman Grande, you might all be dead doornails now."

He had everyone's attentions. They waited for an explanation. None came. He apparently needed prompting.

"What are you talking about?!" Schwietz shouted.

"Talking about? You have not heard?" Mustafa glanced sideways at Schwietz. "A little over an hour ago — Boom! A bomb went off at the Ottoman Grande. Half of the Ottoman Grande is not so grand now. Those still alive have been taken out covered in ashes. Pretty women covered in ashes is not a pretty sight."

He shook his head at the horror of it. "There may be another bomb, they think, in the half of the Ottoman Grande that is still standing. . . You have not heard?! You have no radio?!" He indicated the earplug in his ear. That they did not have a radio appeared as incomprehensible to him as the information he was relaying was to them.

The Americans had no response. They needed time to think. As attorneys they were trained to think before speaking. It might be a long time before any of them opened his mouth. There was just too much happening in too short a span of time. Their brains needed time to digest it all. To make some sense of it — the near plane crash, Esselman getting shot and now the blowing away of luxury at the Ottoman Grande. It was all too much.

Mustafa drove on, circling around some over-turned garbage cans blocking the road, and driving further into darkness where the only light was his one flickering headlight.

A half-hour later, they arrived in front of the ruins of a large, dark, crumbling three story warehouse. It was flanked by similar warehouses. Across the cobblestone road were what appeared to be closed wharfs, with hints of a river behind the wharfs. It was very dark and hard to make out anything. In the distance, a ship's horn moaned like a love-sick hippopotamus.

Mustafa assured them the warehouse he pulled up in front of was a safe place. It certainly looked like a building no one would waste a bomb on.

When the luggage was out of the van, Mustafa cried, "Güle güle!" and sped off without another word.

"Güle güle? What the hell is güle güle?" asked Casey McCall.

"That's goodbye in Turkish," said Weinstein.

The rain was beginning to come down a little heavier. The alternatives were stand in the rain or move to what looked like the door of the warehouse Mustafa said was safe. They lifted their luggage and went and banged on the barn-like door.

After about twenty knocks, the door creaked opened and someone shined a flashlight in their faces.

"We're looking for lodging," cried O'Brien to the flashlight.

"A place to stay!" J.R. said when no answer came from behind the flashlight. "Just for the night."

"Is this a hotel?" Casey asked. "Or we going to say güle güle?"

"Bkz bu otel?" said Weinstein.

A long pause, then an old voice from behind the flashlight said, "Come in."

They took their suitcases up and moved inside.

"Any light in here?" Schwietz asked.

In response, a chain hanging in the center of the room was pulled and a dim light revealed a small room that eleven people and their luggage filled.

"What the hell is this?" McCall muttered.

"This is the lobby of the Warehouse Hotel. Do you want rooms or are you here from the Istanbul *Times* to write a review?" It was the voice from behind the flashlight.

The lobby of the Warehouse Hotel reminded Millie of the parlor of a fortune teller/medium in Atlantic City she had visited years ago with her mother. Her mother went to the fortune teller/medium to get in touch with Millie's dearly departed Uncle Benny, to ask him where he had stashed his last payroll check.

The Warehouse Hotel looked like it had the same decorators as the Atlantic City medium — The room was saturated with red brocade, chintz and gold tassels.

The ageless old man with the flashlight appeared to

be dressed in a white nightshirt. But to Western eyes, Millie realized, what was a nightshirt might be day wear in Turkey.

After pulling the light chain, the old man moved over to a tiny reception desk wedged below a staircase.

"I just want a bed without bugs," mumbled O'Brien. "Where do I go?"

"Five American dollars, sign the register and you go to your room," said the old man.

Everyone got out their five dollars.

* * *

Millie could not sleep. She kept thinking of Esselman, wondering if there were any chance that he was alive. She hated guns. She wanted all guns outlawed. All guns destroyed. How dare anyone be allowed to take up a gun! Why couldn't people just realize people should not be allowed to walk around with guns! Why couldn't everyone love everybody? The world would be a lot safer.

She fell asleep...

She was dancing with a charming young man. They danced and danced. And then she and the charming young man thought it would be a good idea to get married. And they got married and they had a son. The son grew. And the charming young man grew and she grew. . . Only they all grew in different directions.

They weren't dancing any longer. The music had stopped and the charming young man was no longer charming nor young. He had grown fat and balding. And their son had his own friends and he looked on his parents with a cold contempt. And no one spoke to anyone on the rare occasions the three of them ate a meal together. Each was in his own world, with his own projects. And they were all very, very busy succeeding. They had no time to look at each other and nothing to say to each other, even if they had the time to say it.

And then one day, she got a visit from police officers. They were there to tell her there had been an accident out on I-65. The charming young man-that-was and her son would never be coming home again.

There was nothing left in life but what she spent all her time on — her legal practice. She threw herself into her legal practice with a vengeance. Only her work began to appear empty, and as hard as she worked, nothing could stop the tears at night.

Millie passed from dream into that near-awake state. For the briefest of moments it was just a sad dream, then she recalled the charming young-man-that-was her dance partner once and the son they had — that the two of them had names, and she knew their names, but she couldn't bring herself to say their names . . . because she realized, it wasn't a dream. It was her life. It was her life.

And nothing could stop the tears. Only the blue pills could sometimes make her forget for a while.

Sunlight was in her eyes, and she knew she must get up. Get up, put her makeup on and face another meaningless day in a meaningless world. And smile at all the strangers.

She squinted and saw her head was resting on a pink pillow, an ever-so-soft pillow. She could rest here forever. She blinked and realized where "here" was.

Istanbul, Turkey! Of all the silliest places in the world to be! But it was the place she came to escape and forget.

She opened her eyes and looked at a very odd room.

A room she had given no thought to at four a.m. when the old man gave her the key. So tiny a room and yet so high a ceiling. The room was no bigger than a closet and yet the ceiling was higher than the Cathedral's ceiling in River City. The ceiling must have been thirty feet above her. Looked like it was painted white once, but that must have been generations ago. The walls were a tomato red all the way up to the white filigree trim that framed the ceiling.

Nothing in the room but the little rosewood framed bed with pink sheets and braided quilt. No pictures. No mirrors. Nothing. Only a narrow window, narrow in width, but in height it seemed to go almost as high as the ceiling. Faded, ancient white lace curtains framed the sunshine that lit the room. What Eastern mystic or Turkish poet delighted in this very odd room in ages gone by?

Through the closed window could be heard birds chirping and the sounds of people shouting in a foreign language, car horns and ships blowing their horns on the river.

She went to the window. Two little sparrows had a nest on the ledge of the window. They sat in their nest chirping away, oblivious to Millie. Beyond the window ledge was an unexpected spectacle — a road packed with people and vehicles of all descriptions. Was this the same road that was so empty a few hours ago?!

Here were hundreds of dock workers, loading and unloading cargo from lorries and onto lorries. Some lorries were wooden wagons pulled by horses, some were trucks that looked like antiques from the1920's, and some were reasonably modern looking trucks.

The workers were mostly dressed in baggy rags of various bright colors, red, yellow, green predominating. Some wore turbans, others didn't. They all had mustaches and most had beards. The cargo they were unloading and loading was as varied as one might imagine at the central unloading dock of a Big Lot discount store. A lot of crates looked like they were full of produce — melons, cabbages, lettuce, tomatoes. Here and there a crate that looked like electronic merchandize. Crates with Arabic and Oriental writing on them. Crates and crates and more crates and trucks and lorries and dock workers as far as the eye could see up and down the cobblestone road.

In addition to all the lorries, cargo was being loaded also on and off a line of ships. Cranes hoisted pallets up and down. It was the busiest street Millie had ever seen.

It was a magical world to Millie, who lived all of her life in River City and had never seen anything like this. Despite the bizarre incident of Esselman's being shot, and the near crash over the Atlantic, she was glad she came on the Istanbul CLE.

She turned and looked at her odd little red room and smiled. And then remembered the old man had said, when he handed her the key last night, "the bath is down the hall." So what?! It was still going to be a great week of adventure and forgetting. Which is just what she needed. She was going to enjoy the week and get some of the magic Bohnert got from Istanbul. Even without her big blue pills, which they had taken from her at the airport.

It was almost one o'clock when Millie descended the stairs to the tiny lobby of the Warehouse Hotel. She had knocked on a few doors in proximity to hers before coming down and got no answers. Her colleagues must be up and about or still sleeping.

Downstairs the lobby was empty. No one was even at the reception desk. An ancient book lay open on the reception desk, the cover facing up. *The Story of a White Black Bird* by Alfred du Musset. "Harvard Classic 1922" was printed on the spine.

There was a colored glass beaded curtain hanging from a doorway adjacent to the reception desk. Millie hadn't noticed it when they arrived. Her attention was drawn to it by the soft sweet sounds of Arabian/Oriental music, reminiscent of Rimsky-Korsakov's "Schererazade." The music was coming from behind the curtain.

She peaked through the beaded curtain and saw a small dining room. The room was packed with men and some women dining. The old man of the night before, still in his "nightshirt" and a young assistant in white shirt and black pants, seemed to be running around serving everyone. No doubt the lunch time crowd. Many of the men looked like the dock workers. The women, Millie couldn't place; maybe they were friends of the dock workers. Most of the women appeared to be stylishly dressed in Western clothing. Here and there a woman had a scarf on her head, but head scarfs were the exception. Not at all what Millie expected. Maybe the women worked in the warehouse offices.

At one table at the far side, her eye caught four from her party — Weinstein, Casey McCall, David O'Brien and Tom Schwietz. She parted the glass beads and crossed to them.

"Millie! There you are! Come have breakfast," O'Brien greeted her with a raised glass that appeared to be filled with water.

On the table was a large platter with a variety of dishes

on it.

"They have a great breakfast if you like cucumbers, figs, yogurt and Russian olives," said Weinstein.

Casey grabbed a chair from another table and Millie joined them. "The shelled almonds aren't bad, nor the little fried fish with the heads still on them," Casey said. "And the melon slices are the best you'll ever eat."

Casey had a glazed look to eyes as did O'Brien.

"Have you guys been drinking?" Millie asked.

"They have indeed!" Schwietz glared at his companions. "Not a very smart thing to do under the circumstances."

Millie smiled, recalling how much Schwietz was drinking on the trip over and when flying the burning Junker. Maybe it's only okay to drink when flying planes? she was tempted to ask Schwietz.

For a moment, Schwietz reminded Millie of the movie actor Robert Shaw playing a tank commander in an old movie she could not remember the name of. She was almost tempted to ask him, Did he realize how much he looked like the movie actor Robert Shaw? And what was the name of the movie in which he played a tank commander?

"It's raki!" O'Brien held up his drink to Schwietz. "It's the national drink of Turkey. When in Turkey—How about a glass, Millie, my dear." He poured her a glass of what looked like water.

Millie stared at it and thought: It is water and he is going to change it into a magic drink. She looked at O'Brien and never realized till he had some of the national drink of Turkey in him, how much he looked like a leprechaun.

She was not going to have any leprechaun magic potions. She wanted to give Reality in Turkey a try without seeing it through drugged eyes. "Where are the others?" Millie asked.

"Moore went to find Esselman. The good news is Esselman is at one of the hospitals," Schwietz informed her.

"Thank God! That's a relief!" Millie exclaimed. Maybe, just maybe they might be able to enjoy the week after all.

She eyed the platter of food on the table to see if there was anything she might substitute for oatmeal or scrambled eggs. "Do they have coffee?" she asked.

"Do they!" Weinstein smiled. "One cup will get you through the week." He was sipping out of a tiny cup.

"Where are the others?" Millie asked again and took up one of the pastries on the platter.

"Mary Jo's off to find the American consulate. Eh, Fowler went to see someone about dogs." Schwietz looked depressed. "Simon's up in his room, reconstructing his legal brief. They took all his notes and laptop last night, you know."

"He says he's got an appointment later this afternoon with a Turkish attorney to see if he can replevin his 'work product' and laptop from the police." O'Brien laughed and poured himself another raki. He and Casey were studying a map.

"Render is over there." Weinstein nodded.

Millie glanced over at Render in suit and tie staring at his Turkish breakfast with distaste. He was alone.

"We invited him to join us," Weinstein shrugged. "He declined." He shook his head. "That boy is weird!"

"Leave him be. He's a loner like Simon. Wrapped up in his own little world. Lot of famous people have been loners," said O'Brien.

"To hell with Simon. To hell with Render!" Schwietz was agitated. "We have problems."

"Like what?" Millie asked. The pastry was delicious. It wasn't quite a baklava; it had more nuts than a baklava and wasn't as sweet. But it was better than any pastry she had ever tasted in River City.

"There is a whole bunch of unanswered questions," Schwietz said, keeping his voice low.

"Such as?" Millie asked.

"Am I the only one in this crowd that's thinking?!" Schwietz growled.

"You're brain is in overdrive. We're on vacation! Give it a rest!" O'Brien said.

"Yeah, give it a rest! Have a glass of raki and give it a rest," said McCall.

Schwietz ignored them and turned to Millie. "Listen, has it occurred to you that whoever was shooting at Esselman might not have intended his shot for Esselman? He might have been shooting at one of the rest of us."

"Who?" A chill ran through Millie. Was it her intuition waking up?

"I don't know. Anyone of us!" Schwietz shot back.

"That's a cheerful thought," Weinstein muttered.

"If he was shooting at anyone," O'Brien said, "It was probably one of the Turkish businessmen. A dissatisfied customer."

"Yeah," Casey said, "a dissatisfied customer. Got a Turkish carpet that wouldn't fly." Casey and O'Brien laughed.

Millie thought: If I do anything this week, I'm going to get a Turkish carpet.

"You won't be laughing," Schwietz said to O'Brien

and Casey, "if the shooter pops up to finish the job!"

"And then," he continued in a somber tone, "there's the little matter of half of the Ottoman Grande being blown away. It really happened. It's all over today's Istanbul *Times.*"

"Can you relax?" O'Brien asked. "We're not at the Ottoman Grande."

"If we hadn't been delayed at the airport, we would have been at the Ottoman Grande when the bomb went off. Is that a coincidence?!"

O'Brien thought about it a moment and said, "I call it good luck."

"And another bit of 'good luck' was that troop of police and military showing up instantly and detaining us at the airport?! Remember? — And what did that fat police chief mean last night when he said, We think there might be more here than meets the eye?!" Schwietz was finding it hard to keep his voice down.

"He actually said, 'There might be more here than meets *your eyes,'*" corrected Weinstein.

"Yeah, well that's his problem. Fact is, there must be something he knows that we don't," Schwietz countered.

"Tell me: how did he and the other one, that military guy Kamal and all the soldiers just *happen* to pop up so quickly?" Schwietz looked at all of them for one answer to one of his questions.

"You know you're a hell of a guy to vacation with," O'Brien said. "Why didn't you stay home and read mystery thrillers?"

"Yeah, why didn't you stay home and read mystery thrillers?" Casey repeated and sipped his raki and returned his attention to his map.

"And the worst part of all this," Schwietz said to Millie, "is that Kamal character taking our passports and saying we can't leave the country till they get to the bottom of this. Who knows how the hell long that could take?! Investigations can go on for years!!

"These two," he pointed at O'Brien and Casey, "were a little concerned — until they got into the raki."

"Hey, here's the Hellespont!" Casey cried to O'Brien. "That's where Shelly drowned trying to swim across it. No, no, wait a minute, that was in Italy he drowned. The Hellespont is what Lord Byron swam. "

"How the hell to do you know that?" O'Brien asked.

"Sometimes it pays to read," Casey observed.

"How far is it from shore to shore?" asked O'Brien. They searched for a mileage legend on the map.

Casey got a light in his eyes. "Are you thinking what I'm thinking?" He giggled. "And I was going to spend the week looking for a race track and a tennis court."

Millie looked at Weinstein. "What do you thinking, David?"

"I am thinking Turkey is 98% Moslem and a good Jewish boy maybe shouldn't be here too long." He sipped his Turkish coffee.

Schwietz motioned Millie to come closer to him. She leaned across to him. Face to face, he said, in almost a whisper, *"We've got to make plans to get the hell out of here!"*

"Where is Art?" Millie asked.

"That's another mystery," Schwietz replied. "Nobody knows."

CHAPTER 4

Life is a brief dance.
                                                    — a dancer

*T*hey were fully clothed from head to foot in out-of-this-world costumes, large skirts and hats shaped like cones. They spun round and round with their arms outstretched and their heads tilted to one side, as if their necks were broken. Men and women, spinning around, oblivious to the world. Drunk on the dance. Round and round they spun to the gentle beat of tambourines, mandolins, flutes and chanting in an unknown language.

These were the whirling dervish. A branch of Sufi mysticism founded in the 13th Century by Persia's greatest mystical poet, Jalahud-din Rumi.

That they were there watching the dervishes was thanks to Cabot Cabot. Cabot Cabot was the first assistant to the under-secretary at the American Consulate's office in Istanbul.

Cabot Cabot just happened to be on duty Monday afternoon when Mary Jo, J. R. and Larry Simon showed up to see if they could get help in dealing with the Turkish police.

The Consulate's office was basically a trading post. Thorny matters (i.e. anything disagreeable) were referred to and handled by the Embassy, 454 kilometers (290 miles) away in the capital, Ankara.

Still, Cabot Cabot knew his way around the block. He had a few markers he could call in.

Cabot Cabot made one phone call and told his new found friends from River City that Esselman was at Istanbul Central Hospital. Another phone call and Cabot Cabot cleared the way for the Americans to visit Esselman at Central Hospital Monday evening.

Several other calls by Cabot Cabot finally got the police to reluctantly disgorge Simon's legal notepads and laptop and all the cell phones, palm pilots and passports of the River City Americans.

The release of the Americans' property and passports had not been easy. Somewhere down the line, there would be pay-back and Cabot Cabot would be obliged to pull some strings for Turkish officials who might want to get some relatives into the U.S. through the "scholarship diversity program."

Cabot Cabot made this clear to the Americans and told them they would have to pay him back personally by allowing him to show them around Istanbul Tuesday.

Why did a government bureaucrat move with such uncharacteristic vigor and swift effectiveness? He could easily have told them to fill out complaint form number 706 and the Embassy attaché (who always came to town on Wednesdays) would get back to them in due course.

Why did the government official make himself so available for the River City Americans when there were piles of papers on his desk and even other American tourists with problems that needed attending to?

To anyone who was present Monday afternoon at the Consulate's office it was as clear as it was to Millie here Tuesday mid-morning at the Divan Literature Museum watching the Dervishes:

Cabot Cabot was smitten with the red-headed beauty, Mary Jo. He couldn't take his eyes off of her. She watched the Dervishes. He watched her.

* * *

After the Whirling Dervish, Cabot Cabot took his friends to lunch at the posh Golden Ramekin, which had the best belly dancer performer in the world.

A waiter led them to a table with silk white table cloth, close to the dance floor. The party consisted of Millie, Weinstein, Mary Jo and Cabot Cabot.

The dancer was quite an act. In contrast to the overly-clothed Whirling Dervish, the world famous E'mmya wore the bare legal minimum. Where the Dervish appeared to be revolving statues, E'mmya had more moves than a Mississippi eel and could gyrate faster than a jackhammer.

"Belly dancing is an ancient art form," Cabot Cabot explained to the wide-eyed Mary Jo and Millie, who unconsciously held their hands on their abdomens. Weinstein just sat with a smile, enjoying the show.

When the waiter had handed out the menus, and left with the drink order, Cabot Cabot's pager went off.

He apologized. "Can never get away." He mumbled. "Excuse me a moment."

He dialed a number on his cell phone and listened, said "Thank you," and hung up. He sat with a grave look on his face.

Mary Jo asked, "Is everything okay?"

"I had a suspicion; it's just been confirmed." His mood was somber.

The waiter brought the drink order and Cabot Cabot remained silent.

"What do you recommend?" Looking at the menu, Weinstein asked Cabot, who gave no response.

"Cabot?" prompted Mary Jo.

"I'm sorry. I wasn't listening," Cabot replied.

"What would you recommend?" Mary Jo asked.

"Oh. Bring us the lite platter," he said to the waiter.

"Very good, sir." The waiter gave a little bow and left them.

"What's the matter?" Mary Jo asked Cabot. "Is it anything you can tell us about?"

"Kamal was sent to get the Spider," Cabot whispered.

Mary Jo, Millie and Weinstein blinked.

"Could you repeat that?" requested Weinstein.

"Kamal was sent to get the Spider," Cabot whispered.

The three Americans looked at each other. "That's what I thought he said," said Weinstein.

It was as if their charming host had just turned into a bullfrog. Visibly he was becoming more agitated by the moment.

"Cabot," said Mary Jo tenderly, "you're going to have to explain."

Cabot sighed. "There is too much to explain. You told me there was an Inspector Jurice Kamal at the airport when Esselman was shot?"

They acknowledged they did. "He had a fanatic's eyes," Mary Jo added.

"Yes, very fanatic, I'm sure," said Cabot. "I have just learned that Ankara has sent him to Istanbul to get the Spider. I was hoping it wasn't so."

"Who is the Spider?" Millie asked.

Cabot Cabot took out a handkerchief and wiped his

brow. He was breathing heavy. "The number one most dangerous person in the world. Oh, I know that must sound crazy, but I am not exaggerating," said Cabot Cabot.

"The 'Spider' is the most dangerous person in the world, and I don't think any of us has heard of him," said Weinstein.

"You're going to have to take my word that he exists and he *is* the most dangerous," Cabot Cabot replied. "I don't have time to lay out the proof."

"If he's such a villain, why don't we know of him?" Mary Jo asked. The jury was still out on Cabot Cabot's sanity.

"People like the Spider shun publicity. Oh, major media several times were prepared to run stories on him, and then mysteriously — the stories disappeared. Sometimes even the reporters who put the stories together disappeared. You must realize the real world is not exactly as the major media present it to be. There is much, much more, " Cabot Cabot said and took a deep breath.

"Eh, this 'Spider' — He's a gangster?" asked Weinstein.

"Gangster is too mild a term. He's more like a mega-Mafia boss. A gangsters' gangster. A broker for the world's underworld. He's much more effective than the Mafia in blackmail, bribes, intimidation and if blackmail, bribes and intimidation don't work, good old fashion killing."

"Is that his name, Mr. Spider?" Millie asked.

"No. No." Cabot shook his head. "Nobody knows his name or what he looks like. He's called the Spider because he operates like a spider. He's perfectly still and yet his web traps his victims. And his web reaches all over the world. He controls the flow of illegal drugs into Europe and a good portion of the drugs reaching the U.S.

"Slowly, he's been taking over Istanbul, the gateway to the West," said Cabot Cabot. Cabot took out a pill box and a pill, put it in his mouth and reached for his water glass.

"Nobody's working to stop him?" asked Weinstein.

"Officially, he's wanted by Interpol and every police force on the planet. MI5, the CIA, you name it, would like to nab him. That's official. Unofficially, by bribes and threats against families, he has neutralized most of his enemies."

"You said Kamal was sent to get him? Is that a bad thing?" Millie asked.

"It's like sending a devil to get a devil. Kamal got his reputation massacring and torturing Kurds in the Kurdish uprisings in the '80's —another unreported news story. 'The butcher of Lypii' they called him. I can't tell you what he did to the people of Lypii, not if you want to eat lunch."

"Where is Lypii?" asked Mary Jo.

"No longer on any map!" replied Cabot Cabot.

"What has all this to do with us?" Weinstein asked.

"When Esselman got shot — why was Kamal immediately on the scene?" Cabot Cabot challenged.

They had no answer.

"Kamal had to be there because he must have had a tip that something to do with the Spider was happening at the airport. Every move Kamal makes is related to his pursuit of the Spider." Cabot Cabot reflected. "And what happened at the airport?"

"You're saying that Inspector Kamal thinks that Esselman getting shot is somehow connected to the Spider?!" Mary Jo asked.

"Not only Esselman getting shot. Your party was booked into the Ottoman Grande, which was bombed. Nobody has claimed credit for the bombing. A lot of people could have, but nobody did." Cabot's tone was growing urgent.

"Why is that significant?" asked Weinstein.

"Turkey is a political cauldron." Cabot Cabot sighed. "There are a lot of factions that might have boasted they bombed the Ottoman Grande. *None of them have.* None of the socialists parties, nor none of the radical Moslems.

"The Spider, on the other hand, never claims credit. He operates in silence. His actions speak for themselves. The socialists and radical Moslems are loud and noisy. The Spider is not. His silence has been much more effective in conquering by intimidation.

"Because no one else has claimed the bombing as theirs, by deduction, the Ottoman Grande bombing is the work of the Spider.

"To Kamal being at the airport because of a tip on the Spider, Esselman getting shot *and* you being booked into the Ottoman Grande would all be too much of a coincidence.

"In brief, your party is stuck between the crosshairs of the most ruthless gangster in the world and the most fanatical Inspector — who will do *anything* to achieve his goal."

"Are you saying the Spider shot Esselman and blew up the Ottoman Grande because we were going to be there?" asked Weinstein.

"I don't know. But that's the way Kamal probably looks at it. What I am saying is Turkey is not a good place for any of you.

"As much as I'd love you to stay . . ." Cabot was

speaking to Mary Jo, and paused slightly before continuing, "for your own safety, I urge you all to leave Turkey as fast as possible. I can make arrangements to have you all out of the country by this—Oh!"

He stopped speaking as if remembering something and then quite unexpectedly, Cabot Cabot collapsed in his chair.

Mary Jo screamed, and was up at his side, loosening his tie.

Millie and Weinstein stood and rushed around to see what they could do.

"I'll get them to call a doctor," said Weinstein and ran off.

Millie stood beside Mary Jo, feeling helpless. And then she froze. A chill ran through her blood. There he was, again.

He looked like Omar Sharif, Millie's all time favorite actor. He sat at a table twenty feet away, dressed in a black suit, white shirt, and smoking a thin Turkish cigarette. He was staring at her.

It had to be an hallucination. Omar Sharif twenty feet away staring at her? It must be an hallucination . . .because this Omar Sharif look-alike was at the Whirling Dervish performance staring at her.

Their eyes locked. For just a moment Millie felt a flicker of romance.

CHAPTER 5

"Istanbul is a wonderful place to visit . . ."
— Eloise Herrin
God Is Working in Turkey

*M*ary Jo, Weinstein and Millie accompanied Cabot Cabot to the hospital. The Consulate office was notified. Cabot Cabot's American doctor they were told by the consulate secretary would be at the hospital — as soon as he could be located.

Mary Jo, Millie and Weinstein, not being relatives were confined to the waiting room. Mary Jo kept trying to explain to the Chief Nurse that it would be good for Cabot Cabot if she were by his side. The nurse kept shaking her head, and saying repeatedly, "The hospital has protocol. Only immediate family members allowed." It wasn't clear as to whether the Head Nurse knew any more English.

"I know he would want me at his side!" Mary Jo insisted.

"Sorry!" The Nurse shook her head and rushed off.

This was not the hospital they had brought Esselman to. There was no one at this hospital that they had met before.

Mary Jo came back to Millie and Weinstein. "I'm going to try to find someone in charge here and hope they have a brain." That she had deep feelings for Cabot Cabot could not be concealed. She was more emotional than Millie had ever seen her.

"I'm sorry," Mary Jo said trying to conceal her tears. "I'm being selfish. There's no sense all of us waiting here. Why don't the two of you round up the others and get them to the Consulate's office for safety. I'll wait here. I'll be okay as soon as Cabot's American doctor arrives or someone from the Consulate's office."

"I'll wait with you," Millie said.

"No, no. Go with David." Mary wiped her tears away.

Millie knew the feeling of wanting to be alone at a time like this. She nodded. "Okay."

"Wait for the American doctor," Weinstein advised. "Don't rock the boat with the Hospital staff, or you might bring Inspector Kamal and his merry band of men in green down on you."

Weinstein and Millie caught a cab back to the Warehouse Hotel. Luckily, the driver knew how to get to the Warehouse Hotel.

In the cab, after going over all they knew of their situation, Weinstein and Millie sat silent, each lost in his own thoughts with no answers.

Millie was wondering what happened to all the magic of Istanbul that Bohnert spoke of. Being caught between the Spider and the Inspector was not the magic she was anticipating! It seemed like she had fallen from a meaningless universe into a comic book universe. Why should she be apprehensive about a gangster called the Spider and a mad Inspector pursuing him?! What did she have to do with either of them?! All she wanted was a vacation to sort out a purpose to go on living.

Seated in the cab, Weinstein muttered, "Ferrari!"

"What?" Millie wasn't sure he said anything.

"Ferrari —That's what he shouted before he shot Esselman."

"Was it?" Millie couldn't see that it mattered much; the results were Esselman was shot.

"I was the closest to him," Weinstein continued. "At the time it didn't register what he shouted. I was focused on the fact he was shooting at us. Now I remember. It was 'Ferrari!' Wasn't it?" He looked at Millie to confirm it.

"I couldn't say. It could have been," Millie conceded. "I wasn't paying attention. I was thinking about getting my pills through customs. If it was 'Ferrari' what does it mean?"

"It's a car," Weinstein said.

"I know that! But why would he shout 'Ferrari' before shooting Esselman?" Millie asked.

"I don't know," Weinstein mumbled and fell silent.

It was about five p.m., Tuesday evening, when they arrived at the Warehouse Hotel.

The street appeared empty. The dock warehouses were closed. They asked the cabbie to wait.

The barn door to the Warehouse Hotel was open. The old man in the nightshirt was at the desk under the stairs. He was smoking a hookah pipe, (the kind with the hose that had the smoke going through a globe full of water, and gave off a very pleasant forget-all-your-troubles aroma).

He was reading. Millie recognized the cover. It was his Harvard Classic of 1922, Musset's *The Story of a White Blackbird*. He noted their entrance with a cold nod and returned to his book. They nodded back and went up the stairs.

Knocking on all the doors on the second floor brought no answers.

Only Larry Simon was in his room. He was working

away on his never-ending legal memorandum. He had no idea where anyone else was. "They didn't tell me when they left or where they were going."

Weinstein and Millie told Larry all that Cabot Cabot had told them at the Golden Ramekin — about the Spider and about Inspector Kamal. And how it was Cabot Cabot's advice that they get out of Turkey ASAP.

"We're here to round up everyone and get them to the American Consulate's for safety," Weinstein said.

"I think not," said Larry. "We're here to attend a seminar tomorrow at the University of Istanbul. And then we have a few days to ourselves.

"I, personally, have an appointment with some calligraphy specialists on Thursday." He gave a half smile as if confessing to a secret vice and turned serious again, "And I happen to like the quiet seclusion of the Warehouse Hotel. I don't like brou-ha-ha. I'm staying put."

"Larry, I don't think we've made the situation clear to you. You might get a lot of 'brou-ha-ha' if Inspector Kamal has the idea we are connected to the Spider—"

"I'm not connected with any spider," Larry chuckled. "Though there may be several spiders lurking near the ceiling in my room. Isn't it amazing how high the ceilings are. Is your ceiling as high as mine?" Larry opened his door, inviting them to a better view of his ceiling. He looked up himself, squinting as if to see whether there was any spider activity at the moment.

Weinstein was in no mood to play look at the ceiling for spiders. "Larry, this Kamal guy is called the Butcher of Lypii!"

Simon lowered his gaze from the ceiling to look at

Weinstein. "David, every town has a butcher."

Weinstein looked at Millie. "You try!"

"Kamal will seize all your yellow pads, Larry," Millie said, "and he'll ram them down your throat and throw you into a dungeon!"

Simon gulped, possibly at the thought of his yellow pads going down his throat, but the next second he was smiling. "He wouldn't do that. I got everything back after it was explained who we are and what we are doing here."

"That was Cabot Cabot's doing. There's no Cabot Cabot now to protect us," Millie said.

"Stay here and you won't get to the seminar or to visit with your calligraphy playmates," added Weinstein. "You'll be chopped liver!"

"I'm an American citizen," Larry said. Like that said it all. "My 'calligraphy playmates,' as you refer to them, are experts who happen to have a deep admiration for my penmanship!" (Simon did all his writing in the neatest block letters produced by human hand.) His mind was set on what his mind was set.

"Kamal will torture you to get at what he thinks you know till the American Ambassador arrives to say a word — over your mangled body!" Weinstein was almost shouting.

"We must let the law take its course, David," Larry said calmly. "We must never avoid legal authority. To avoid legal authority is to show a disrespect for the law and to invite chaos, societal disintegration."

Simon raised his chin and pulled down the bottom edges of his vest. "Now, if you will excuse me, I have work to do before dinner." He shut his door as quick as one of the three pigs when confronted by the big bad wolf.

It was useless.

Back at the front desk, they asked the concierge if he had seen any of their party. He knew nothing of their coming or going. "Are you staying another night? It will be another five dollars."

It was now about six. Weinstein and Millie left a note at the desk for the others to go to the American Consulate's building at once, where an explanation would await them.

They packed up their own belongings and checked out of the Warehouse Hotel and had their waiting cab drive them to the American consulate's office.

The consulate's office was closed. No one was home. The lights were out. It was about six-thirty p.m.

Luckily, the cab was still waiting outside the consulate's building, a modest stone structure on a street with many office buildings.

"I could have told you they would be closed," the cabbie said. "They are always closed on Tuesdays. Sometimes they open at noon on Wednesdays, sometimes they don't. Depends on whether there have been any bomb threats."

"Why didn't you tell us that on the way here?!" asked Weinstein.

The cabbie shrugged, "You didn't ask. I go where people tell me to go. Maybe they know something I don't know. If I tell them where they want to go is closed — they get out of my cab. I lose a fare. So why should I tell them where they want to go is closed? You tell me. Unless directly asked, why should I tell?"

"What are we going to do now?" Millie wondered.

They decided to go back to the Warehouse Hotel and retrieve their note. It would make no sense to direct their colleagues to the Consulate's building if it was closed.

"Why don't you call and tell the concierge to rip up the note?" asked the cabbie.

"Have you been listening to our conversation?!" Weinstein was indignant.

"What do you think cabbies do?!" The cabbie matched Weinstein's indignation. "When passengers speak, do I have ears or not? What am I to do with my ears? Plug up my ears and not hear emergency vehicles that may wish to go around me? Would you like me to cause a big accident because I have plugs in my ears so I should not hear you?!"

"He's right," Millie said. "We've been babbling away like he didn't exist. It's our fault."

"But I do exist, and I am particularly listening when I hear you speak of Inspector Kamal and the Spider," the cabbie said.

"Oh God! Now we're in for it!" moaned Weinstein.

"You're not going to turn us in? Are you?" asked Millie.

"Turn you in? Why would I do that? No. No. If you are in trouble with either of them, you are fighting Great Evil, and you can count on Izzy," he said.

"Who is Izzy?" asked Weinstein warily.

"Me! I am Izzy," said Izzy, the cab driver. He tapped his breast and turned to offer his hand to them. He wasn't driving. They were sitting in his cab outside the Consulate building.

"Izzy, we're not fighting anybody. We're simply trying to save our skins," Weinstein said.

"That my friend, is impossible. What did your Mr. Ben Franklin say — He who chooses security over freedom will lose both."

"We're not equipped to fight anyone, Izzy," Millie said. "We didn't come here to fight. And now —We just want to get out of your country."

"Oh no!" Weinstein was almost in a panic.

Izzy and Millie turned to see what had Weinstein's attention. In front of them, four police cars and a small armored personnel vehicle were pulling up in front of the Consulate building. Army troops were getting out of the armored vehicle and standing in front of the entrance to the Consulate building.

"This is bad news," muttered Izzy and turned on the ignition and slowly edge the cab into the evening traffic. Fortunately, they weren't parked directly in front of the Consulate building and did not draw the attention of the police and soldiers.

That evening they spent in Izzy's apartment.

Izzy was a mid-thirties bachelor who lived in a very poor neighborhood on the side of a hill. Istanbul is built on seven hills, like Rome. And some of the hills of Istanbul are graced with palaces for the tourists and some are covered with over-crowded slums for the Istanbulis.

The cab belonged to Izzy and he parked outside the apartment building he lived in. The narrow street was filled with children playing among a forest of over-flowing garbage cans. The children appeared as happy as if the garbage cans were tree stumps in a forest.

Women in cheap black dresses were hanging out windows, presumably keeping an eye on the children. Here and there a window box with herbs or flowers graced a window, and a clothes line hung across the narrow street.

The four story high buildings looked like they were made of adobe mud, vaguely similar, Millie thought, to the deserted Indian villages in the Southwest of the United States she had seen on her honeymoon. The man who-was-no-more loved the Southwest.

Inside the building Izzy lived in, the red clay walls were not plastered. Izzy's apartment, on the second floor, consisted of two small rooms. Babies cried from all the other apartments.

Izzy's apartment was as small and as messy as any bachelor's pad the world over.

Weinstein and Millie didn't mind. They were grateful to have a place to hide while they figured out their next move.

Izzy cut some hard cheese and put it into pita bread with a grape leaf. This was dinner. The drink menu had two offerings: brackish rain water collected on the window sill or kefir, a yogurt-like drink with reputed medicinal properties and a legendary lore that went back, according to Izzy, to the Bible's Manna. [Exodus 16 :31. As the Israelites wandered in the desert, God fed them with a sweet white substance, supposedly the kefir grains, which fell from the Heavens.]

While they ate, they discussed their options.

"There must be more American official contacts in Istanbul than the Consulate's building!" Weinstein said. "If we could somehow get in touch with American authorities."

Izzy said, "Yes, you could call the American Embassy in Ankara or go to one of the American air bases. Plenty of American presence in Istanbul and Turkey. And you can go to them and hope the American authorities do not turn you over to the Turkish authorities. . ."

"They wouldn't do that?!" Millie protested.

"First thing the American authorities do when you tell them your story is check with the Turkish authorities to confirm it," Izzy explained cutting more cheese. "Turkish authorities say, 'Yes, these people are material witnesses in a crime scene.'

"Unless the people who run to the Americans are very, *very* important — I mean strategically important — they are turned over by the Americans to the Turkish authorities. I've seen it happen too many times," Izzy shook his head and offered them more cheese.

"Why would they do that?!" Millie exclaimed.

"You don't understand? Really?! Your government very much wants to keep Turkey happy. To keep Turkey aligned with the West, and not to join with the Islamic world. You do not know, Turkey is 98 percent Moslem? American backing here is razor thin and only sustained by millions of American dollars that prop up the secular government."

"I don't think we realize anything," Weinstein said. "And we don't want to and we have no time to. We only realize we are in doo-doo, way over our head. *And we want out.*"

To Millie and Weinstein if the American "authorities" turned them over to the requesting "Turkish authorities" —it would mean they would be in the hands of Inspector Mohammed Abul Mohammed and Special Army Inspector Jurice Kamal, the butcher of Lypii.

Millie recalled how early Monday morning Mohammed Abul Mohammed had ordered that they were not to leave the country till the shooter of Esselman was apprehended and brought to justice.

Attempting to leave the country might be interpreted by Inspector Mohammed Abul Mohammed as "interfering with official police business." Which Inspector Mohammed Abul Mohammed informed them carried a twenty year sentence in Turkey.

"The cheese is good," said Millie, to relieve the gloom. "What is it called?"

"It's airag," said Izzy.

"It's delicious." Millie took another piece.

"Thank you," Izzy said. "It is my favorite."

"What is made of?" She bit off a piece.

"Fermented horse milk," Izzy said.

Millie put the cheese down and forced swallowed what she had in her mouth. She made a mental note to never again ask where anything she liked came from.

"What do we know for certain?" asked Weinstein. "Let's review."

"We arrived and Esselman got shot," said Millie.

"And the police and Kamal mysteriously appeared on the scene immediately," Weinstein added.

". . . Cabot Cabot told us Kamal was sent to get the Spider. So . . ." Millie said. "So where are we?"

"According to Cabot Cabot's thinking, Kamal could only have popped up so immediately when Esselman got shot because Kamal had some tip that something to do with the Spider was going to happen at the airport," Weinstein said. "And when Esselman got shot—it somehow in Kamal's mind — tied our group to the Spider. Do I have it right?"

Millie nodded her agreement. "And don't forget the coincidence that we were booked into the Ottoman Grande on the night it got bombed! We all told the Inspectors when interviewed that we were staying at the Ottoman Grande. So when they heard it got bombed, they must have thought somehow we were involved, especially after Esselman getting shot.

"Cabot Cabot," she continued, "who has been on the playing field here a lot longer than us, said we should all get out of Dodge as quick as possible or have the Butcher of Lypii rounding us up to torture us into revealing our connection to the Spider . . . It all sounds so crazy! And we're on the run for doing nothing!"

"Perfectly normal in Turkey," Izzy put in his two cents. "But what is— where is this 'Dodge' you have to get out of?"

Millie explained "Dodge" was just an idiomatic expression. Turkey is what was intended.

After a moment of chewing on his pita sandwich, Weinstein said, "You know, that's *Cabot's analysis.* And I'm not questioning it, but at bottom — we haven't done anything. They've got to realize that! I'm more curious as to whom the shooter at the airport was shooting at. Maybe Schwietz is right, maybe it wasn't Esselman."

"I'm wondering where everyone is!" Millie cried. "If we could just get everyone together, I'd feel a lot better."

"Well, we know where you and I are — I think —," replied Weinstein, looking around at Izzy's shabby apartment.

"Don't worry, you're safe with Izzy!" Izzy assured them. "No one ever comes down this street unless they absolutely have to. If the police came down this street, it would make news. It would be a revolution."

"My guess is Mary Jo will be at the hospital till Cabot Cabot is released," Weinstein continued. "Simon is at the Warehouse Hotel. . . Esselman is presumably still at his hospital. . ."

"Do you think the police or Kamal have picked up the others?" asked Millie.

Ignored, Izzy turned on his television.

It caught Weinstein's and Millie's attention. Millie was surprised there was a T.V.; it was a little model in a purple plastic shell, almost like a toy. It was nestled in mounds of dirty laundry.

"Excuse me, while I catch the news," Izzy said. "In Turkey it's always good to know what is going on."

Millie and Weinstein turned again to trying to figure out where the others in their party might be.

Monday evening, after they all visited Esselman at the hospital, J. R. expressed an interest in seeing the Kapalicarsi, the world famous covered bazaar of over 4,000 shops. Slim chance of finding J.R. in such a labyrinth. He could be there or visiting Esselman or anywhere.

Monday evening, there was no word from Fowler who had gone off to see friends about dogs, but didn't give anyone anything more specific.

Schwietz, Weinstein recalled, was very agitated about getting a plane to fly them all out, and he mentioned he might have a friend at an American air base somewhere in Turkey. The odds were Schwietz went to an air base. . . which ever base that might be. . .

Izzy put in there were several American air bases. "But remember what I said about American authorities turning people over to Turkish authorities."

"O'Brien seemed hell-bent on finding the best bar in Istanbul, and Casey McCall seemed to be right behind him," said Weinstein.

Izzy said there were many, many "best bars" in Istanbul.

Render. . . Well, he could be anywhere, anywhere you can stare into space.

"And what happened to Chalmers?!" Millie asked. "He's the one who put this together?! If anyone should be answering to Turkish authorities, it's him! Where is he?!"

"Nobody has seen him since we checked into the Warehouse Hotel," Weinstein said. "He didn't even come with us to see unconscious Esselman. No one has seen or heard from him."

Izzy laughed drawing Millie's attention. It was a news report on the television. The report was in the Turkish language. On the screen police were hauling up a young man from the river bank. They threw a blanket around him and escorted him to a police van."

"Oh no!" said Millie. "We don't have to wonder where Casey McCall is any longer!"

Weinstein rushed to watch the television.

"You know this funny person?" asked Izzy.

"I guess Cabot Cabot was right," Millie muttered.

"No," Weinstein said. "This has nothing to do with the Spider or Kamal."

"How can you say that?! He's under arrest!"

"Sssh . . . He's being arrested for attempting to swim the Hellespont," said Weinstein.

"How do you know that?!" asked Millie.

"That's what the announcer is saying," Weinstein said.

"How do you know?! Ever since you interceded on my behalf about my pills at the airport, I've wondered — When did you learn Turkish?!" Millie asked.

"Nadar Shunnarah taught me a little." [Ed. Note: Shunnarah was the master of languages in the Hall. It is said he could teach anyone any language in five minutes.]

Weinstein was still focused on the television.

Confronted with two amazing facts, Weinstein's learning some of the Turkish language from Shunnarah and Casey McCall being arrested for trying to swim the Hellespoint, Millie turned to the immediate one playing out before them:

Casey was shouting, "I could have done it! I could have done it! If you goons didn't interfere!" They watched as he was unceremoniously pushed into the police van and the doors were slammed and the van drove off. The Turkish reporter said a few more words in Turkish, and the picture on the screen switched to the anchor couple, a man and a woman who smiled and spoke some more in Turkish, and then the picture switched to an interview with someone talking, apparently about something else.

Millie turned away from the television. "Why would Casey want to swim the Hellespont?!" She was dumbfounded.

Izzy looked at her in bewilderment. "You do not know the legend of Hero and Leander?!"

Millie was lost. She turned to Weinstein.

"Don't look at me!" Weinstein responded, "I had a public school education."

Izzy sighed and told them the ancient Greek legend about Leander every night swimming the Hellespont, now called the Dardanelles, to see his love, Hero, a priestess in Sestos.

"The Elizabethan playwright Christopher Marlowe wrote a play about them, *Hero and Leander,* and the romantic English poet Lord Byron — you are familiar with him, no?—

wrote *The Bride of Abydos*— about Hero and Leander. Byron also swam the Hellespont, himself," Izzy said. "I can't believe you do not know all this!"

Millie and Weinstein looked at Izzy with blank expressions. "You think Casey was trying to duplicate Byron and Leander's swim?" asked Millie.

"Why would he do that?" Weinstein wondered.

Izzy shrugged. "People do crazy things. Many others have come to Istanbul to swim the Hellespont so they could say they did what Byron and Leander did. I don't know why they do it. But then, I do not know why people climb Mountain Everest, or why in Turkey we have camel fighting in Selcuk or olive oil wrestling. Or why they have a rattlesnake roundup in a place called Opp in your country. There are many things I don't understand. But I accept."

"Camel fighting? Rattlesnake roundup?! A place called Opp?! — You're making all that up, aren't you?" Millie said.

"I wish I was." Izzy shook his head in the negative.

"I had a case once involving a Ferrari," Weinstein whispered.

"What?" Millie asked switching her attention back from Izzy to Weinstein.

"The shooter at the airport was shooting at me!" Weinstein exclaimed.

CHAPTER 6

"All nations before him are as nothing;
and they are counted to him
less than nothing, and vanity."
— Isaiah 40:17

He was seventy plus and at least fifty plus over-weight, which on a five foot frame gave him the appearance of a living beach ball. His dress underscored the beach ball effect: baggy red pants, a plaid jacket, a yellow checkered shirt, and an over-sized puffy red bow tie.

He had a deep sonorous voice that took long pauses in which air was laboriously sucked into the beach ball. He had the standard Turkish bushy black mustache and bushy eyebrows on a beefy face. A cheap toupee sat precariously atop the beach ball and a red fez with gold tassel sat on the toupee; if he moved too fast, the toupee/fez combo might be on the floor.

But he didn't move too fast. In fact, aside from breathing and speaking, and slowly turning pages on his speech resting on the lectern, he didn't seem to move at all. He did list to the left, which suggested he might be a globe instead of a beach ball.

This was the world-renowned Professor Hafaaz, whose lecture entitled, "World Government and Parking Tickets," had brought twelve River City attorneys halfway round the world.

It was not just the River City attorneys who signed up to hear Professor Hafaaz. The Istanbul University lecture hall was filled with people wearing glasses who appeared to be from all over the planet. There were Europeans, Orientals, Latinos, Africans, and Arabs. All very studious. People that looked like they lived in their heads. In international circles, Professor Hafaaz came with impeccable credentials, in which outward appearance was of no account.

The good Professor oozed mind-boggling abstractions: "Over-population, technology that allows for the management and accomodation of over-population, the potential for mass destruction, the social and economic chaos caused by disfunction in a single nation or region of the global economy — are *some* of the conditions compelling the world to an inevitable one world government. A world government that under the present circumstance, will most likely be the United Nations."

Millie sat in the back of the lecture hall, searching the crowd to catch sight of anyone of the River City party.

"It will be a government that holds all civil liberties not as unalienable rights from God as declared in the American Declaration of Independence, but all freedom as granted by the United Nations. In order words, your rights come from a human institution, not God.

"This is a critical point. The United Nations, the world government to come, will not be run by saints. Like all democratic governments, it will be a mechanism for the majority of the have-nots to feed on the haves, or what is euphemistically referred to as 'distribution justice.'

"It will be socialistic by impulse, values and rhetoric and dictatorial in practice." Professor Hafazz droned on.

It was Wednesday morning.

Yesterday, when Cabot Cabot had his heart attack at

the Golden Ramekin, seemed light years away.

Millie was alone now. Last night when Weinstein became convinced the shooter at the airport was after him, he had Izzy drive him down to the Bosporus. Izzy had friends there who would take him to the European side, where he possibly could catch the Orient Express. Or maybe he could get a small boat to smuggle him to Greece or Bulgaria. Once in another country, he could approach the American Embassy without having them throw him to the Turkish police. It would be too much paperwork for someone who was only a witness and not the criminal. All of this advice from Izzy.

Millie chose to stay in Istanbul and make one last effort to round up the others. Weinstein was too worried about the shooter coming after him over a Ferrari.

"When world government comes, it will come as a logical, reasonable necessity. But there will be nowhere anyone will be able to escape the penalties of local ordinances violated — of *any* jurisdiction that one has visited anywhere in the world.

"If you neglected to pay a parking ticket in Grenada, for instance, your license will be suspended in *your* country and community of residence —until you satisfy the demands, however outrageous, of the jurisdiction where you failed to pay the parking ticket.

"Computers talking to each other and the internet make all of this possible, and very profitable for the jurisdictions."

Millie had no intention of ever getting a parking ticket in Grenada. Halfaaz was enough to put Millie to sleep again. She had to stay awake and alert, though. She was searching the audience for any of her friends. The only one she could spot was Larry Simon, sitting under the nose of Professor

Hafaaz. No use talking to Larry, Millie thought. Where were the others?!

Was it just a coincidence that Cabot's heart attack came right after he told them about Colonel Kamal and the Spider? Who was the Spider?! And why should Colonel Kamal think they were involved with the Spider?!

Was the shooter at the airport shooting at Esselman or at Weinstein? Why did he shout "Ferrari"?

Was it a coincidence that the Ottoman Grande was bombed? Was it her imagination or was the Omar Sharif look-alike at the Golden Ramekin staring at her? The same Omar Sharif look-alike staring at her at the performance of the Whirling Dervish. (She hadn't mentioned the Omar Sharif character to Weinstein; he might think she was nuts. And maybe she was!)

Weinstein's imagination, Millie thought, might be running wild, too. Because he had a divorce case ten years ago in which a Ferrari was at issue, why would someone pop up and shoot at him in Istanbul?!

Where were all the other River City attorneys?! Did Colonel Kamal have them in custody? With Cabot Cabot in the hospital, who would be there at the Consulate to rescue them? If they could even get through to the Consulate's office. All phone attempts only got the answering machine.

"Parking tickets are emblematic of the difficulties and webs of legal structure that will burden all citizens of the world. The law of the world will be our master. And the law of the world will be as all law, a fist. One size fits all. Except when graft or nepotism ameliorate. If one is to consider...." Professor Hafazz droned on.

Millie was beginning to feel nauseous. The room felt

overheated and confining, but no one seemed to mind.

Men in black trenchcoats entered and began walking up and down the aisles looking at the audience. Were they searching for her and her colleagues? Millie slouched down and tried to hide her face in a bibliography handed out at the the entrances.

"Every item of commerce today has a barcode; it is a great convenience for commerce. Today it is being asked: Why not a barcode on every person? What a greater convenience for multiple reasons. . ." Hafazz paused to have a coughing fit.

One of the the men searching the audience looked in her direction. She put her face down and pretended to have a coughing fit.

She could take no more. Abruptly, she got up and left the lecture hall with her fake cough as a pretext. She did not look back to see if anyone was following.

Izzy was waiting for her just outside the University. "Glad you are here. I almost got a parking ticket," he said.

They went to the hospital where Cabot Cabot had been taken. Millie was told he was no longer at the hospital and they could give her no further information as to where he might be. The hospital spokesman said they knew nothing of a redhead name of Mary Jo Wicker. "You might want to check with the police," the hospital spokesman suggested.

Millie didn't want to risk going back to the Hafaaz lecture. What was she to do?

She was in a near panic state. Maybe she should have gone with Weinstein last night. "I haven't done anything wrong! All my friends have disappeared. I can't find any of them!"

Izzy suggested they make one last visit to the Warehouse Hotel. Out of desperation, she agreed.

As they approached the Warehouse Hotel, the cab pulled abruptly to the curb. Millie was about to ask why, when she saw what Izzy saw: Three police cars, a police van and a small crowd of policemen were outside the Warehouse Hotel a few doors down the street.

The police were taking out the concierge in handcuffs and several others Millie could not identify. Next came police with their arms full of — suitcases! Millie was positive she could see the suitcases of her colleagues.

How dare they! She had an impulse to jump out of the cab and run up to them.

Were any of her colleagues already in the van before she arrived?

"We should get out of here!" said Izzy. "But we can't drive around that," Izzy said, indicating how the police cars and van had blocked off the street.

"Turn around then," said Millie.

" This is a one way street. It would draw immediate attention," Izzy said.

"What then?" Millie asked.

Izzy did not answer, but in a minute he made a decision. He slid to the passenger side of the front seat, opened the door and got out of the cab, and started walking away from the Warehouse Hotel.

"What?!" Millie didn't know whether she should follow him or not. Some soldiers or police, whatever they were with the black boots and machine guns, noticed Izzy. One of the soldiers pointed and shouted *"Almak onu!"*

Izzy began to run.

A soldier raised his machine gun to fire at Izzy.

"Yok! Almak ornu!" shouted someone to the soldiers.

The soldiers ran after Izzy, right past the cab. Millie ducked down in the back seat, hoping they didn't catch sight of her in their focus on Izzy. Was that Izzy's plan? To divert attention from her?

When she heard no more soldiers running by, she waited a moment and then slowly rose up to see— Colonel Kamal glaring at her through the windshield of the cab. He shouted at his soldiers and they hauled Millie out of the cab.

"This time, your Consulate friend is not going to safe you!" Colonel Kamal said to her when they brought her face to face with him.

"What right have you to—!"

Colonel Kamal slapped her across the face. *"Almak onu!"* He turned and got in a police car, and his driver did a U-turn and sped off, the wrong way on a one way street.

The other police vehicles followed leaving only the police van and a couple of soldiers by the van.

The soldiers hauled Millie off to the van.

They reached the van, opened the van door and were about to push her in with the others, when the soldiers hesitated. Their attention was drawn to a mob across the street. Millie had noticed them out of the corner of her eye before and assumed they were just dock worker spectators.

The mob was approaching the soldiers. The soldiers holding Millie drew back and let go of Millie to raise their guns.

The mob came on faster. Clubs appeared and were raised and the mob began chanting, *"Olarka ile zulum!"*

The soldiers hesitated a moment, dropped their guns

and ran down the street, abandoning Millie and the van.

A victory cheer went up from the mob. Some of the mob ran after the soldiers. Some overwhelmed and began beating one of the soldiers who had stood his ground, apparently too petrified to run.

Those who had been taken into custody began getting out of the van. Millie looked to see if any of her River City colleagues got out of the van, but none did. Just men that looked like dock workers and women dressed in Western dress.

Soldiers or police were returning with Izzy. There was a moment of indecision in which both the soldiers and the mob stared at each other. The soldiers hesitated. There were perhaps ten soldiers and at least a thousand in the mob. The mob charged the soldier. One soldier raised his gun, but decided not to fire. Instead, he turned and ran down the street with the other soldiers, who abandoned Izzy.

Many cheers went up when the soldiers ran. Some returned to the van and some ran after the soldiers.

The concierge from the Warehouse Hotel and several mob leaders were arguing. The concierge appeared to be mad about something.

Some of the mob were inspecting the suitcases taken from the Warehouse Hotel by the soldiers. Others were being embraced by the detainees released from the van.

The concierge caught sight of Millie and pointed at her and went around to the various mob leaders, now intent on opening the suitcases. Yelling and pointing at Millie, the concierge managed to get the mob leaders' attention on Millie.

Millie began backing off; perhaps this was not the best time to mention some of those suitcases she believed belonged to her colleagues.

The mob leaders began closing in on her. There was nowhere for her to retreat. She was very soon at the center of a closed circle of mob leaders and the concierge still shouting.

One of the mob leaders snapped at the concierge and it silenced him. The mob leaders began appraising Millie as if she were a piece of fresh meat.

Soon the mob leaders were arguing among themselves; Millie guessed that it might be how to carve her up.

From nowhere, Izzy drove his cab up close to where the mob leaders were with Millie. He got out and pushed his way into the closed circle and began talking to the mob leaders. Whatever he said, it gave the mob leaders more fuel for discussion.

A cheer went up from some rioters around the van.

It caught everyone's attention. Someone held up a set of keys and jumped into the van. Everyone applauded. The police van was their property now. As were all the items in the suitcases which were being opened by various rioters.

The leaders, still surrounding Millie, Izzy and the concierge, turned their attention back to Millie, and began arguing with Izzy again. It was getting nasty.

Another distraction: someone came running up shouting. Whatever it was, it put fear into everyone.

Mob leaders and all ran down the street. The concierge ran into the Wharehouse Hotel and shut the door. Izzy got into his cab.

"What is it?" Millie asked.

"Many more soldiers are coming! Quick, get in!"

CHAPTER 7

*"No other piece of geography on earth
has been home to so many different people
over so many centuries."*
— Stephen Kinzer
Crescent & Star

$\mathcal{T}$he cab was his and they could go wherever he wanted. And they did.

When they were well-away from the Warehouse Hotel, they stopped at a phone booth and Millie made a bunch of quick phone calls with no results.

She wanted Izzy to drive her to the American Embassy in Ankara. Phone calls only got the answering machine saying, leave a message, we'll call you back.

The American Consulate had a similar message, and the Consulate itself was still guarded by Turkish police.

Cabot Cabot was transferred by his physician to an undisclosed location she was told when she phoned the hospital. The hospital could not tell her where. The hospital knew nothing about a red-head lady.

With great reluctance on Izzy's part, she had him drive her back to the University, in hopes she could find someone — *anyone* — even Simon — from her group. But she caught no sight of Simon; maybe they already had him and his precious legal notes in custody.

The lecture hall was closed; a student informed her there was a lunch break. She caught sight of police and soldiers going around checking I.D.'s. She quickly left the campus. They might be Colonel Kamal's men, sent to round up the Americans.

"You must get out of the country, Mrs. Sharp," Izzy insisted.

"What about the Embassy?!" Millie said.

"You could try for a run to your Embassy. It is in Ankara, which is close to three hundred miles from here. All along the way, there could be check points. Your picture could be posted at those checkpoints. . ."

"Could I just get on a plane somewhere and fly out?" Millie asked.

"Ten years ago, yes. Today, with technologies' efficiencies, there is a very good chance your picture could be posted at every seaport, every airport, at every border crossing. I am not exaggerating. Copy machines and fax machines have made pictures very easy to distribute."

* * *

The rest of the day was spent in the cab. They drove out of Istanbul. At first, they went south. At Izmit, they turned west. "They will not expect you to go this route. They will be looking for you to make a dash for Bulgaria or Greece," Izzy said.

So westward they went. Izzy said he had a reliable friend in a small fishing village where the Dardanelles opens to the Mediterranean. His friend, for a price, could get her to Israel, where she would be able to make contacts to get her back to America.

They spent the day going westward along the coastal road that wound through mountains overlooking the magnificently peaceful Sea of Marmara. They passed modest farm houses, and drove through small villages that seemed to be inhabited only by women dressed in black lugging water jugs in the sun and old men sitting in the shade playing chess or backgammon and sipping raki.

At one village, when they had to stop for gas, Izzy advised Millie to cover her head and face with a makeshift veil. The Moslem sentiments against Western women ran very strong in that particular village, he told her. Indeed, in most of the countryside.

They passed various ruins: a Roman amphitheater, a Byzantine fortress, and the rubble of what the archeologists said, according to Izzy, was once a Hittite village.

"The Hittites are mentioned in the Book of Genesis several times," Izzy commented as they drove by the Hittite village ruins. "But to those who think the Bible a fairy tale, the Hittites never existed — till archeologists found them — a great empire stretching all across Turkey."

At each ruin, Millie had to resist the temptation to stop and walk around, to see what it would feel like to stand where people had stood two and three thousand years ago. She had majored in history and here it was literally passing in front of her eyes and she could not stop and touch it. The whole countryside was one great outdoor museum.

They did not have time to sight-see. They had a destination — the small seaside village where Izzy's friend with a fishing boat would take her to Israel, out of the hands of Colonel Kamal. Millie hoped there was an ATM machine in the seaside village.

"Are you going to go to Israel, too?" Millie asked.

"I am an Istanbuli! I am a Turk! I will not leave my city or my country! I take this drive for you," Izzy said.

"I appreciate that. But won't they come after you for

helping me?" Millie asked.

He shrugged. "I may have to . . . How do you say in your American gangster movies, 'lie low till the heat blows under —' or is it 'blows over.' There are plenty of places to hide in Istanbul if you are an Istanbuli. Not so if you are an American housewife."

"How do you know I am a housewife?" Millie regretted asking as soon as the words were out. She didn't want to get into her personal life.

"Are you not?" Izzy asked in surprise.

"Yes," she admitted and to herself, she added, "I used to be . . . at least in name."

"You have children, yes?" Izzy asked innocently.

"I had a son. He. . . died. . . in a car accident." She could hardly get the words out. She shut her eyes and took a deep breath to check the tears. She had no blue pills.

"I am very, very sorry. Automobiles are very dangerous. I always try to drive as carefully as possible," he said, and slowed down.

They drove on in silence for about ten minutes.

"What about yourself?" Millie asked. "You're not a husband, judging by your apartment."

He laughed. "No no. No woman would have me. And if there were one that would, I would be very suspicious of her. I have nothing to provide for a bride."

"Izzy! How can you say that? What if your father—" she began.

"Don't tell me about my father!" Izzy cried. And then in a softer voice: "My mother could not even tell me if he was Greek, Rumanian or Bulgarian. Or maybe he was Polish or Syrian. She told me he knew a lot of languages and he was a fast talker. And a faster traveler — He deserted my mother when she was pregnant."

"I'm sorry," Millie said.

"You have no reason to be sorry," Izzy said, "unless you somehow are related to my father."

"What?" Millie saw in his rearview mirror he was smiling. She smiled back. "You must have had a great mother."

"Yes, she was. Unfortunately, I did not appreciate her till it was too late. Like my father, I ran off and left her."

He told her how at sixteen he was infected with wanderlust and left his mother. After many adventures in Eastern Europe, trouble with the police in Rumania, Bulgaria, and Greece, after trying various ways of making a living, some legal, some not, and not liking any of them; and after many, many women, and much sorrow, he finally came back to Istanbul, and found his mother had passed away. He had no family. Nothing. But finally he discovered happiness and freedom in driving a cab. The cab was his. It was his life. He could go wherever he liked, which is why he could leave Istanbul and drive her hundreds of miles along the coast.

"So you see," he concluded, "I have nothing to offer any woman. And if I ever found one who was unfortunate enough to want to be with me, who is to say that when she became pregnant, I might be just like my father and run off. I would not want to do that to anyone, especially to one who wanted to be my wife."

"You do have one thing to offer a woman," Millie said.

"What is that?" He was suspicious.

"A ride in a cab." She smiled and he laughed. "And I

bet if she were pregnant, you'd get her to the hospital before you had to deliver the baby in your cab."

"You are a crazy American!" He laughed.

They drove on in silence.

Millie looked out the window. The Sea of Marmara stretched out for as far as the eye could see from the vantage of the winding mountain road they were traveling. Millie wished she could be on one of the yachts or sailboats thousands of feet below. Soon — when they reached the village where she could get passage to Israel —she would be.

"Who owns all those beautiful boats?" she wondered aloud.

"Some are rented out to tourists from all over. Others are the property of the rich from all over. Mostly Europeans. The coast of Turkey is one of the most beautiful, unknown vacation places in the world," Izzy replied, adding almost to himself ". . . If you can forget the government and some of the people. . ."

Millie was staring at the placid sea, and wondering how many ancient ships might be lying a few hundred feet below the surface at any given point, perhaps some spot of water her eyes were on.

Out of the blue, Izzy asked, "You really do not know the Spider?"

The question surprised her. "So help me God!"

"No one seems to know who he is," Izzy sneered. "But his influence is everywhere."

"Everywhere?" Millie challenged.

Izzy looked at her through his rearview mirror. He seemed to be saying, How dumb is this lady.

"You do not know — almost ninety percent of illegal

drugs in Europe come through Turkey?" he asked.

She recalled Cabot Cabot had said something about the Spider and the drug trade at the Golden Ramekin.

"The cocoa plants are grown in Afghanistan and smuggled through Turkey, without much trouble, and from Turkey, 'somehow' they make it into the hands of all the crime lords of Europe." He took out a pack of cigarettes and offered her one.

" No, thanks . . . And the Spider is responsible for all of the illegal drugs in Europe?" Millie was skeptical.

"He used to have competitors, but they have all disappeared." Izzy lit his cigarette with a lighter. He looked from one side of the road to the other, as if to see if anyone was hiding, listening to what he was saying in the open afternoon sun.

"Drugs are only part of the Spider's business," he continued. "He has also been involved in brokering the sale of uranium from the former USSR across the Black Sea into the hands of certain parties in the radical Moslem world."

"If that were true, I would think the C.I.A. would be all over him," Millie said.

"All over him?" He frowned.

"After him," Millie said.

"Oh. They are. As is Interpol, and all the governments of Europe. They are all 'after' him. Way after him." Izzy was bitter.

"Tell me about Kamal." Millie always tried to see the good side to everyone. Despite the smack he gave her across the face earlier in the day, she was trying to find some good in him.

"Ask Maslova."

"Who is Maslova?" Millie asked.

"She is a very attractive young lady down the hall from me —you know where I live. She is very attractive except half of her face is burnt off.

"She was a child in Lypii, when Kamal and his men came. They thought Maslova's father might be helping the Kurdish rebels. Kamal's men broke into their house in the middle of the night. They made Maslova's father witness his wife and daughters being raped and shot. And then they drove a spike though his head. Little Maslova — she witnessed it all hiding under a table. If they had seen her they would have killed her. They didn't see her. When they were finished they torched the house, which is how Maslova got half of her face burned off."

"That is a horrible story," Millie muttered.

"There are Kurds and Armenians in Istanbul who can tell you worse," said Izzy.

They drove on in silence for a bit. Millie finally asked why the Turks were fighting the Kurds. Izzy gave her a brief summary of how a few years back the Kurds had tried to establish their own cultural identity in Turkey and how they had been brutally suppressed. Colonel Kamal was one of the commanders responsible for the atrocities, which mostly never got reported.

"If they weren't reported, how do you know about it?" Millie asked.

"In Istanbul, there are many Kurds without eyes, legs or arms who escaped the massacres and tortures in the east," Izzy said.

"What about the Western press?"

He shook his head. "You are so naive. Turkey is an

ally of the West. Your country has betrayed the Kurds more than once for the sake of her alliance with Turkey. Your country needs Turkey, first against the USSR and then against Iraq, and now for strategic alliance against Moslem radicals."

Millie had no response. She did not like to hear what he was saying. International politics and intrigue was not a subject she was ever interested in. It was certainly something she didn't feel she could do anything about. Just keeping up with being a competent family law attorney helping wronged housewives was enough.

"Oh, Jesus, Mary and Joseph!" Izzy cried.

At first Millie thought he was praying. Then she saw he was looking in his rear-view mirror, slowing down and pulling to the side of the road.

She quickly turned to see an army truck coming up fast behind them.

The cab came to a stop on the gravel shoulder. The army truck sped by so close to the cab, the wind wave in its wake rocked the cab. Another truck was behind the first, and then a third. And then silence. Silence, except for a bird squawking from a branch of a dead tree seemed to be laughing at them; to Millie, the bird looked very much like a vulture.

Slowly, Izzy took a deep breath and drove the cab back onto the road. Thereafter, he kept checking his rear-view mirror.

* * *

Another half hour or so and they were on a plain with nothing on either side. The sun was going down. There was nothing around, not even a bird sitting on the branch of a dead tree.

Millie was just about to ask, How much longer, when up on their right there was a sign, with one word of it. Millie yelled, "Stop!!!"

Izzy pulled the cab to the side of the road. "What?"

"I want to go there!" Millie pointed at the sign.

Izzy looked at the sign. The one word on the sign in English and several other languages was: Troy.

"You want to go to Troy?! We don't have time!" Izzy yelled.

"I don't care. I want to see Troy. If you will not take me, I will get out here and walk." Millie said and put her hand on the door handle.

"All you Americans are crazy!" Izzy said in disgust and drove the cab on to the dirt road that headed to the right.

The road was bumpy and there were tall grasses on both sides and boulders. Ten minutes off the main road, looming up was a mound of rubble that covered many acres.

How could she begin to explain her need to see Troy?

Izzy stopped the cab.

"Is this as close as you can get?" Millie asked.

"I have a flat! In case you haven't noticed!" Izzy got out and went to the rear of the cab.

"I thought it was the road," Millie said.

"It was this damn road that gave me the flat! Well, there is your precious Troy, go run around it, play on the rubble while I fix the flat! It will be dark in less than an hour. Get your fill!" Izzy was taking out a jack and tire from the trunk.

"Thanks," Millie said and started off toward the mound that was once Troy.

"Watch out for the snakes!" Izzy called.

CHAPTER 8

*"So was the dread fray of Trojans and Achaians left to
itself, and the battle swayed oft this way and that across the
plain, as they aimed against each other their bronze-shod
javelins, between Simoeis and the streams of Xanthos."*

— Homer
The Iliad, Book VI

*S*he wished he hadn't mentioned snakes. She would
be thinking snakes instead of experiencing.

When she was twelve, she read Homer's *Iliad,* and
then another book on the excavations that found Troy. Millie
yearned to see Heinrich Schliemann's excavations; she was
sure that if she could stand on the spot, she would know
whether it was the real Troy, and if the real Troy, that all that
Homer told was true.

It was a twenty minute walk from where Izzy and the
cab were to where the ruins began.

She walked among the cold stones, here and there a
bit of stone blocks suggested where a wall once was. And
then a precipice. She was standing on what could have been
a wall. Below was a plain. The plains of Troy. The Scamander
plain. In the distance, the sea.

Could this have been the view Helen had of the
Achaian (Greek) army and their camp by their ships? Was it
from this vantage the Trojans first caught sight of the armada,
which had come to avenge Paris' stealing Helen away from
King Menelaos? How much the Trojans must have hated the
woman that brought this disaster on them.

Millie walked on to another spot, two walls at right

angle and a stone bench. Was it here that Hector and Andromache said their last goodbye before Hector went out to fight Achilles? Was it here that Hector's son was frightened by his father's helmet?

The sun was hovering just above the sea. It was growing dark. She knew she would never have this opportunity again. She wanted to stand on the plains of Troy. She rushed down the rubble, found some stone stairs leading down. The ground was rough terrain of gullies and tall grass. She ran as far and as fast as she could. Toward the sea, to get to some point in the plain where battles were fought. Was it here that Patroclus was cut down by Hector? Were these grooves in the dirt made by Achilles' chariot as he dragged Hector's body around the walls of Troy?

Millie stood lost in time. What it must have been like to have lived in an age where valor in battle was all there was to existence. And people believed in gods and goddesses that took human form and were just as subject to passions as humans.

She imagined herself a Trojan warrior with helmet, shield and spear standing in rank, awaiting the Greeks to come over the ridge between her and the sea.

Or to be one of the Achaians who had sailed for months over the "wine-dark" sea to stand on this plain and look up at the topless towers of Ilium.

She was lost in time and wonder.

Suddenly, there was a loud cracking sound and something whizzed past her head. A hand rose up and pulled her screaming to the ground as another cracking sound followed the first.

Millie found herself lying in a trench with her legal

colleague from River City, Art Chalmers. She kept screaming. Chalmers put his hand over her mouth. "You want to get
yourself shot?" he whispered.

"Hmm?!... Hmm!..." She couldn't get a sentence out.
His hand was firm on her mouth. She began shaking.

"Sssh," Chalmers said. "I'm going to take my hand
away from your mouth, if you will keep quiet," he whispered.

"What the hell—?!" She cried when he took his hand
away from her mouth.

He put his hand over her mouth again. "Sssh! You'll
give away where we are!" he whispered. "Please. I am going to remove my hand again, and I will explain. You promise you won't cry out?"

Millie nodded her head. He released his hand. She
took deep breathes, waiting for his explanation. But no explanation came.

"Ahhh," Chalmers moaned. He sat back in the trench.

"Well?!" asked Millie. She crawled over to him, and
almost screamed again. Chalmers had both his hands over
his chest, and blood was oozing through his fingers. "Oh,
God!" Millie whispered.

"Looks like I've managed to get myself shot." He
examined the blood dripping from his hand. "I don't think
I'll have time to explain. . . " His voice came as a wheezing
sound.

"Art!?" Millie was in tears.

"Sssh," Chalmers whispered, slumping to his right
side. "There are others here, too."

"Who? Is everyone from the CLE here ?!' Millie
whispered.

"No. No. Just me. The others are over there. Unfriendly others." His breathing was labored.

"Unfriendly others? Who?!" Millie was madly trying to orientate herself to the situation. "We've got to get you to a doctor." Millie stated the obvious.

Art smiled. "Very practical, but very impossible." He slumped over in the trench, blood bubbling up from his chest.

"Oh, God! Oh, God!" Millie whined. She tried to stop the blood with her scarf.

"Keep your voice down, Millie, dear!" he whispered. He stuck a stick into his mouth. "It's up to you, now kid."

"Up to *me?!* What's up to me?!" Millie almost shouted.

"Ssssh! Please!" He slumped over further.

"What is going on?!" Millie had the urge to grab him and shake him till he gave her a sensible answer.

"It's all complicated, and I don't think you'd understand or approve, but I do owe you a very big apology," he said. "Which I give you now."

"An apology?! For what?" She looked around as if the answer would be there somewhere beside him. There was only a handgun beside him. The sight of the gun shocked her. She wanted to ask him what was he doing with a handgun. But there were more pressing questions to be asked. "An apology for what?!" she repeated.

"For talking you into coming to Istanbul. . ." his voice trailed off.

"Talking me into coming to Istanbul?! What has that got to do with anything?!"

"No time to explain." He bit on the stick. Between his teeth. "Listen closely. I don't know what brought you here. Maybe the gods. But please, get to the others. . . Tell them. . . ." He trailed off and slumped over.

"Get to the 'others'? The 'unfriendly others'?!" She was lost.

"No, no. Not them!" Art whispered in pain, "Get to..."

"Get to who-them?!" Millie leaned into his face.

He coughed. The stick dropped from his lips and blood flowed from his mouth. "In Istanbul —The Comfort Zone," he whispered. "I'm sorry, Millie. I got you into this. . . Tell them the Spider—" He was lying on the ground.

"Got me into what? —*The Spider?!*" She wanted to shout at him but only whispered it. There was so response. She shook him. "Got me into *what?!* Tell 'them' the Spider —what? What about the Spider?! Who is 'them'? What is the Comfort Zone?!"

His body was still.

Somewhere in the dark, voices were shouting in a foreign tongue to each other. A spray of gunfire strafed the top of the trench.

Art was dead. There was no point staying beside him. Millie crawled quickly toward the ruins of Troy, or at least in the direction she believed she had come. The sun had set and there was no moon or starlight yet to give any clue.

The foreign voices seemed to be moving about on the plain and shouting to each other.

She crawled as quickly as she could. They would get to the trench. They would find Art's body. But they had seen her and they were sure to search for her.

She moved as fast as she could. When she guessed she might be far enough away, she stood up and moved a bit faster, but still cautiously, not wanting to bump into anything that would make a noise and give away her presence.

How much ground did she have to cover to get away?

The ground sloped up; it must be the ruins. Where were the stone stairs she had come down? Should she go right or left? Or should she go up the slope? She went up the slope and ran into a wall. She almost cried out, but knew any noise from her would only bring bullets in her direction.

Which way to go? She said a prayer and went to the right. A few yards of holding to the wall and stumbling over large rocks, and she almost fell completely over the bottom step of the stairs that went up.

With bruised knees and a twisted ankle, she eagerly started up the stairs, almost on hands and knees. She looked back after about twenty steps when she heard one of the voices on the plain cry excitedly.

They must have discovered Chalmers' body. And she could tell there were at least five of them because there were at least five flashlights waving about now perhaps twenty-five yards away.

If one of the flashlights shone in her direction. . .

She moved up the stairs as quickly as she could. She might have made it to the top and away if, in front of her, she hadn't heard a hissing sound. She screamed.

The flashlights below found her, shouts went up, and bullets began ricocheting off the stones. A splinter of stone hit her in the left eye and she screamed again and reflexively moved fast up the steps. Snakes or not, she'd rather get bitten than riddled with bullets.

The flashlights were all over her and bullets were pelting and ricocheting off the stones all about her. She felt a pain in her right calf, as if someone had taken a bite out of her. Was it the snake or a bullet? She kept moving as fast as she could.

The dim light from the flashlights revealed a snake without a head. Blown off by a bullet? She scrambled up the steps. Her left shoe went flying.

They were coming after her fast. She would never be able to out run them. Among the ruins, she found a crack in a wall and made a quick decision. She squeezed into the cold, dark crevice and awaited her fate from snakes, spiders or gunmen.

When Troy fell, when the alarm went out that the Achaians were within the city gate, slaughtering in the night, did any Trojan hide in this very same stone crevice, Millie wondered.

The flashlights came on fast, and the hollering in a foreign tongue. If only she had had the foresight to learn some basic Turkish from the Hall's language master, Nadar Shunnarah as Weinstein had, perhaps she might be able to understand what the men with flashlights searching for her were shouting. But how was she to know she would be hiding in the night in a cold dark crevice in the ruins of Troy? Bohnert did not mention hiding in cracks in walls as part of the "magic" of his trip to Istanbul.

The flashlights and hollering went on for sometime. At one point, light passed over the crevice she hid in and someone's voice was so close, she felt she could have reached out and touched the speaker. She held her breath. The light passed on. The hollering went off in another direction.

She could not say how long it was, but finally the flashlights and hollering disappeared and she was left alone in the cold night.

Was it in a crevice like this that Helen hid as Troy burned? Perhaps, she was standing where Helen stood when Trojan Prince Aeneas discovered her and drew his sword to slay her. But his mother, the goddess Aphrodite, made him put up his sword.

An hour or so later, Millie peeked out and saw the Milky Way galaxy as she had never seen it before. Only in Arizona and New Mexico, not in River City or any modern city, could the majesty of the universe be seen in such clarity.

She was cold, she was hungry, she was bruised, she was frightened, and still —staring up at the vast overwhelming magnificence of the Milky Way, in a strange way she felt . . . almost comforted. She must have stared at the Milky Way for hours, marveling at every shooting star.

It was almost daylight, when she took a chance and crept out from the crevice. No one was around. She stood alone in a dead city. She thought of going back on to the plain and seeing about Chalmers, but then she thought about Izzy. Had he taken off?

She left the ruins and retraced her steps searching for the path back.

Finally, she found the dirt road that led to where Izzy and the cab would be. She hobbled down the road as fast as she could, hoping the men with flashlights were not coming behind her.

In the first light of morning, she could make out the cab up ahead. Bless him, Izzy hadn't left. He was slumped over the wheel! Fell asleep waiting for— No, no. Not napping. Oh, God! His throat was cut. Blood was all over. And the cab, for all the bullet holes, was a piece of Swiss cheese on flat tires.

CHAPTER 9

"Life is a cabaret, old chum!
Come to the cabaret!"
— John Kander & Fred Ebb
Cabaret, the musical

*T*he room was all polished glass and glitter from chandeliers, table lamps to silver and gold armrests on the mahogany barstools. The mirrors behind the bar and mirrors and pyramids of china around the room magnified the effect. A band played music that was fast and loud, a strange mixture of every style of music imaginable. And everyone at every table seemed to be thoroughly enjoying themselves. Waiters carried huge trays, banquets and bottles. Corks were popping all over the room.

A party of well-dressed revelers entered, and almost everyone in the room stood and applauded. A maitre d' rushed to escort them to a center table. All eyes were on the handsome people and applause continued till everyone in the party was seated.

All eyes focused on the celebrities, and no one caught sight ot the creature in rags caked with mud that limped down the stairs from the lobby in the wake of the celebrities. Neither the coat check girls nor the reservation greeter spotted the creature. They had left their posts and entered the dining room to applaud the celebrities.

It wasn't till the creature in rags and caked with mud was standing at the foot of the stairs, that the reservation taker's

nose made him aware someone was there that should not be.
"How did you get in here?!" The screener snapped.
Fearful of losing his job, he gingerly took hold of the creature's
left arm with two fingers in a lobster grip (not wanting to get
himself soiled) and began propelling the beggar up the step
to the lobby. His intention was to throw the baggage back on
the street. How in heaven did this "thing" get past the doorman? Emile, the doorman, too, must have been distracted by
the celebrities, to have let this get in.

"Get your hand off me!" shouted the beggar.

There was apparently a woman of sorts beneath the
mud and rags. "Madam, let us not have a scene." The screener
almost had her into the lobby.

"I don't want to go into your crummy restaurant, I
just want to see if I can locate some friends!" cried the beggar.

"I'm sure no friends of *yours,* madam, are here! I
suggest you try the International Red Cross or the Sisters of
Mercy out on Akentz Cad." He had her almost to the front
door. Emile could handle her once he got her outside.

Getting her outside was the problem. She began to
struggle, and some of her caked mud was flying everywhere.
"Please, would you just check for me! I'm looking for —
Dave!!"

Coming through the revolving door of the restaurant,
Millie couldn't believe it: — It was David O'Brien, with a
blond bombshell by his side.

Millie made a lunge toward O'Brien, but was held
back by the reservation taker. "Dave! Dave!!" she cried.

O'Brien looked around to see who was calling his
name.

"Dave!" Millie cried as she was being dragged to the revolving door.

The blond bombshell caught sight of Millie being pushed through the revolving door. "You have clients even in Istanbul?! I'm impressed."

O'Brien looked puzzled. "Not that I know of. She probably has me confused with another Dave. They entered the restaurant proper and a round of applause greeted them.

"You have fans in Istanbul. I'm impressed," O'Brien said and began escorting the blond bombshell toward the table of the celebrities in the middle of the dining room.

At the same time, Millie circled around the revolving door back into the restaurant lobby and made a dash for the dining room, shouting, "O'Brien!!"

The reservation clerk was right behind her and caught and grabbed her just when she was on the heels of O'Brien, who whirled around at his name being shouted.

"My apologies, Mr. O'Brien," said the reservation clerk.

"Dave! It's me! Millie!" She struggled to get free of the reservation clerk and the two waiters who had come to his assistance. They would easily have been able to drag her off, but not wanting to get soiled by the creature's dirt, they couldn't get a firm hold on her.

"Millie?!" O'Brien looked closely at her. "What happened to you?!"

An hour later, Millie, cleaned up —thanks to attendants in the ladies room —was sitting with O'Brien at the bar.

David Weinstein, to Millie's surprise, was also there.

Millie recounted to them everything that had happened

to her, the death of Art Chalmers, and how she had barely escaped. How she hid among the ruins of Troy while men with submachine guns and flashlights searched for her; how she waited till it was almost daylight before creeping out of hiding and finding her way back to the cab. Only to find, the men with machine guns had found Izzy and left him in a pool of his own blood.

She recounted how she spent the rest of the day getting back to Istanbul, riding in the back of farm wagons carrying sheep and goats to market.

"I should have gone on to that small fishing village and searched for Izzy's friend with a yacht who could have got me to Israel. But Art said get back to the Comfort Zone in Istanbul and 'warn the others.' I wasn't sure what I was to 'warn' you about, but he mentioned the *Spider* — and he apologized to me! I had no idea where the Comfort Zone was or what it was . . . and ..." She almost yelled: "What the hell is going on?!"

"I wish we could tell you, Millie," Weinstein said.

"You don't know what all this is about?! Or you just won't tell me!?!" Millie cried.

"Let's say a little of both," O'Brien said. "But have a glass of raki. It'll calm you down." He signaled the bartender.

"Don't you think we should be getting on the move?" Weinstein said.

"Before I move an inch, I want to know: Why did Art apologize to me for getting me to come to Istanbul?! What am I supposed to 'warn' you about?! And what has the *Spider* to do with all this? And *you!*" She focused on Weinstein, "You were going to escape to Greece or Bulgaria.

What are you doing here?!!"

"Millie, we don't have the time to answer those questions and this is not the right place," O'Brien said, and finished his drink.

Weinstein stood up. "I owe you this, Millie: I was going to escape to Greece or Bulgaria. I just stopped in here for a drink to get my courage up and ran into O'Brien. He explained some things to me."

"Well, explain them to me!" cried Millie.

"No time now. We've got to go!" O'Brien said and put money down on the bar for the drinks.

"Where?" Millie asked. The bartender put an eight ounce glass of a clear liquid in front of her. She was very thirsty. She drank and gagged. "Ahhh! Water here is—"

"Raki is an acquired taste," O'Brien conceded.

"We're not going to be around long enough for her to acquire the taste. We've got to go!" Weinstein urged.

"Alert the others," O'Brien said, "I just want to take a moment to say goodbye. Get Millie out to the car, I'll join you in a minute."

"I'm not going anywhere till I get some explanation!" Millie was almost shouting. If it weren't for the music, others would be turning to look at her.

"Come on, I'll explain what I can on the way," Weinstein said.

O'Brien had walked over to the table of celebrities.

"Who are those people?!" Millie asked.

"American actors and playwrights. There's a festival of American theatre in town," Weinstein said. "Millie, we should go."

"Can I get a sandwich or something? I think I still

have some money left." She opened her purse. which she had the presence of mind to retrive from Izzy's cab.

"Millie, please," said Weinstein.

"No!" Millie pulled her arm away. "I'm tired of being pushed and pulled about. I'm not moving till I get some answers! And some food."

Truth was, she was exhausted, she was hungry, and for all she knew Weinstein and O'Brien had been involved in the killing of Chalmers.

Anything was possible! The past three days had proven that! This place was the first pleasant environment she had been in since arriving in Istanbul — warm, well-lit, a room full of happy people. It seemed highly improbable that anyone was going to burst in and shoot up the place. Even if Colonel Kamal showed up with his storm troopers, he could only be there to enjoy the party. She felt safe sitting at the bar and surveying the happy crowd in front of her. The place is aptly named, she thought. It truly is the Comfort Zone.

"This is not the time for answers," Weinstein said almost in a whisper.

"I can see that," Millie agreed. The bartender placed a platter of hors d'oeuvres in front of her that made her eyes widen. Nuts, fruits, pastries, cheeses, olives, and a dozen other selections, many of which she had no idea what they were, but they all looked so eatable. "What's that!" she asked the bartender.

"Schnecken," the bartender replied. "It's one of our favorites. A specialty of the house. Would madam care for another glass of raki?"

Madam had not realized she had polished off the eight ounce glass of raki, which a moment ago she couldn't stand the taste of. She must have been really thirsty! She nodded her head, "yes," to the bartender as she devoured the schnecken pastries on the platter. It was almost as good as Heitzman's bakery back home.

This was the way her Istanbul holiday was supposed to be! She felt warm and happy, and — okay maybe at the moment she was a touch insane; which a part of her brain told her she was entitled to be. Eat as much as you can and enjoy as much as you can while you can, a voice within said, because tomorrow you will be as Art and Izzy, dead, dead, dead.

She swiveled on her barstool to Weinstein standing beside her; exasperation written all over his face. "Okay, Davey, spill the beans, tell mama all about it!" she said with her mouth full of schnecken.

Weinstein looked like he was about to spill the beans; he actually, began, "I don't know how much I can tell you without— It's really O'Brien that should. . . fill you in . . .as much as. . . as can be told at this time."

Millie's eyes shifted from Weinstein, as he hesitated. She focused on the table of celebrities O'Brien was laughing it up with. They were the playwrights and actors in town for the Festival of American plays, Weinstein told her.

Well, if Millie knew anything about theatre people it was that more than any people in the world, they knew how to enjoy life. And Millie was badly in the need of some enjoyment, some laughs. And there with them was O'Brien who could explain all.

She got off her barstool, and started toward O'Brien and the table of actors and playwrights. "Hold that thought," she said to Weinstein, and was off weaving through the crowd, her replenished glass of raki in one hand and a schnecken pastry in the other.

Weinstein followed after her. "Millie, where are you going?"

"Talk to O'Brien," she replied. "He can explain, you said." And before Weinstein could object, she was standing in front of O'Brien and the table of American theatre celebrities. "Hi!"

"Millie!" O'Brien stood, surprised.

"Aren't you going to introduce me to your friends, Dave?" Millie said.

"Sure. Everybody, this is Millie Sharp, a brilliant attorney and good friend from River City."

"You're Mary Krause!" Millie exclaimed, recognizing the blond O'Brien had arrived at the Comfort Zone with. "I saw you do that one woman Shakespeare show at the Palace!'

"You have a good memory," Mary Krause smiled. "Performers live for moments like this — audience members remembering."

"Pull up a chair," said one of the celebs, "you can help us settle an issue."

"You're R. J. Atkinson! I saw you on Broadway in that musical about Gawain and the Green Knight!" Millie gushed. "You were *very* good!"

"Waiter, another drink here for the beautiful lady who recognizes true talent!" R. J. Atkinson called out.

"To hell with Broadway, help us settle the dispute— Which play was the best in the Festival?" insisted someone else at the table.

"No, no, the question is which play connected with

the audience," interjected another.

O'Brien was beginning the introductions, "Millie, these are the playwrights: Bruce Feld, Tom White, Louis Phillips, Christian Garrison, Jules Tasca."

A short man with a short curley black beard, who had been hovering close by, interrupted the introductions: "The *real* question is how can American claptrap have anything to say to the agony of the Turkish soul?"

Everyone at the table turned and looked at the buttinsky and groaned.

"Are you still here?! Why doesn't someone open a window and let the gnats out?" said one of the playwrights.

"I'll give you agony in your little Turkish soul!" another playwright said and raised a fist.

"It is clear, none of you are Shakespeare!" cried the short man and threw his drink into the face of the playwright confronting him.

A volley of drinks from the playwrights drenched the brave little critic, who began shouting, "You are all a hundred percent swine!"

"And you're a hundred percent wet!" said R. J. Atkinson and poured a decanter of raki over the critic's head.

Others from adjoining tables were drawn into the "discussion," and a snowball began rolling down hill picking up momentum and magnitude. More and more people began shouting, hurling insults and shoving each other.

"You know, that's one of the great thing about Istanbulis," O'Brien observed. "They are genuinely concerned about ideas and every night have a free, lively and open discussion."

"Who is that little man?" asked Millie of the all-wet

bearded fellow now exchanging blows with the playwrights.

"A serious theatre critic, no doubt." O'Brien looked at his watch. "Well, time to be going," he announced cheerfully. He stood up, kissed Mary Krause on the hand. *"Auf Wiederschen, ma chère."*

"Vaya con Dios, my Davey darling," the great actress replied, and blew him a kiss.

O'Brien pulled Millie out of her chair by the arm and across to the bar.

" *'Davey darling'*?!" Millie eyed O'Brien in a new light.

O'Brien turned to Weinstein. "Where are J. R. and Fowler?"

"Have no idea. Just tried to reach them but they're not answering" Weinstein shouted back above the music and shouting.

O'Brien brushed a screaming patron waving a playbill aside and pulled Millie along. The three of them, Weinstein, Millie and O'Brien made their way across the dining room without incident.

What Millie could gather from the confrontation at the celebrities' table, which spread across the dining room, the issue seemed to revolve around the American plays and whether they were right for Turkey.

At the steps leading into the lobby they were confronted by someone who mistook Millie for one of the actresses. He was applauding wildly, "Excellent performance!"

Another patron shouted into Millie's face, "If you had any respect for Turkey, you would have changed out of your costume!"

O'Brien pushed the man back and with Millie and

Weinstein pressed on into the lobby.

At the revolving door, a man with a knife blocked their way and challenged them: "Bring us plays like Giraudoux's *'Sodom and Gomorrah'* or his *'Tiger at the Gate,'* and Anouilh's *'Ring Round the Moon'* or Mary Chase's *Harvey!* And bring us Sarah Bernhardt and Steve McQueen or don't come back!"

Weinstein pushed the man with the knife into a compartment of the revolving door. The three Americans went into another section of the revolving door and revolved around to the street. On the street side, Weinstein broke off a branch from a bush by the door and wedged it into the revolving door, stopping the door from revolving and trapping the man with the knife. He kept shouting at them as they walked away.

There was a crowd across the street that took notice of them.

"Oh, my god!" Millie mumbled.

"Fans of the American theatre?" Weinstein wondered.

"We don't have time to ask," O'Brien said, "The car is this way."

They began walking down a narrow, unlit street away from the Comfort Zone. The crowd of about a hundred began following them.

"Maybe they think we're playwrights and actors." Weinstein said. "And they just want our autographs."

The crowd grew closer, despite the three Americans moving faster. The crowd began shouting something at them.

"What are they shouting?" Millie asked Weinstein.

"I don't think they liked the production," Weinstein replied as the crowd came closer.

"Can't you tell them we had nothing to do with the

plays?!" Millie shouted back.

"Keep calm," said O'Brien. "The car is.... Where is the car?"

"Are you sure it was this block?" Weinstein said.

"I'm not sure of anything, but I think we'd better make a run for it!" cried O'Brien.

The crowd came on faster as the three attorneys from River City ran down the cobble stoned street that seemed to get narrower and darker. Only Millie couldn't run so fast. Her right ankle was still not functioning. Her running was no more than a fast limp dance.

Millie stopped trying to run. O'Brien and Weinstein stopped, too. The crowd stopped running and after a moment started approaching them again slowly, as if wary of any tricks the Americans might have planned.

"Don't be heroes," Millie said. "You guys can get away."

"No, we'll stand together," O'Brien said.

"Besides," added Weinstein, "There is no 'away' to get to from here!"

A stone wall was behind them and the mob surrounded them on three sides.

"We're Americans!" Millie shouted at the crowd.

"That might not be our best selling point!" Weinstein said. *"Dost! Dost!"* Raising his hands, he cried at the crowd.

"What does that mean?" O'Brien asked.

"I think it's suppose to means 'friend.'" Weinstein replied.

There was a groan from the mob and then as an ocean wave, the mob moved in with a roar on the three Americans.

O'Brien and Weinstein did their best to push the foremost of the mob back, but there were too many.

Three big men started pulling Millie away from her companions. She began screaming, and O'Brien and Weinstein started punching at the guys who had hold of her.

Others punched and grabbed at O'Brien and Weinstein. Each of the them was surrounded and separated from the others. In a few brief moments, Millie knew, all three of them would be dead on the sidewalk, stripped of all identity, a footnote in tomorrow's Istanbul *Times,* perhaps next to a review of the American plays.

CHAPTER 10

"There is always a mosque a few steps away
from you in Istanbul."
— a travel agent's report

*T*he crowd began pulling Millie this way and that. She was the last hot item on the shelf at Christmas time. From their cries, it sounded like Weinstein and O'Brien were getting similar treatment. The crowd was separating the three Americans from each other and maybe about to separate some limbs, too.

Someone started yelling something. Millie's head was down as she was being hit and pulled at. She thought maybe the cries referred to her and her companions.

Growls came next. Growls?!! Growls as from dogs. Were they going to sick dogs on them?!

No. There was something else going on. The mob seemed to lose interest in her and turned their attention in the direction of the growls.

These were the sounds of actual dogs! And the dogs were apparently increasingly distracting the mob from ripping the Americans to pieces.

Millie had no idea what was going on. It was too dark to see and she was afraid to lift her head and get another blow to her face. She did hear Weinstein yell, "Fowler! Where have you been?!"

Fowler?! Teddy bear Fowler?! If there were dogs coming to the rescue, they had to be led by Fowler.

Something was happening that had the crowd's attention. Millie could not tell what.

A hand came out and took Millie's hand. It seemed to be a friendly hand. It didn't seem to want to rip her fingers off. The hand gently pulled her away from those whose attention was turning to the dogs. It seemed unreal, but from what Millie could hear, it sounded like the dogs were barking — barking rhythmically in unison. And then she thought she heard someone yell, "They're dancing!"

Millie went with the hand that held her hand and resisted the impulse to stay and see the dancing dogs. The hand took her out of the crowd. Was it Weinstein or O'Brien leading her away? It was too dark to see. And she didn't want to draw anyone's attention by saying anything.

The sounds of the mob and the musical dogs — if dogs it was! — faded, as if they were coming from down the block.

"Where are we going?" Millie whispered to whoever was guiding her.

In response, another hand, presumably the complement of the hand holding her hand, put something in her hand. The hand holding her hand let go of her hand.

She was standing alone in the dark holding something. Whoever put something in her hand disappeared down the street. She was too exhausted to go after him, and was too distracted by the sensation that he had left something in her hand. It felt like a piece of thick paper.

Behind her the dogs had stopped "singing." The crowd had stopped listening. It sounded like chaos was reestablishing itself. The dogs were starting to growl now and the crowd was heating up to anger again.

In another moment, while Millie stood hesitating over which way to go, she could hear louder growls from the dogs and shouts and screams from the crowd. Sounds of scuffling and fighting going on back there. Millie moved in the opposite direction, down the dark street to she knew not where.

And then there was light. A dim street light on a deserted boulevard ahead. The narrow street she was on came to an end at the cobble stoned boulevard.

Alone on the boulevard, under the street light, Millie opened the piece of thick paper that had been deposited in her hand by the stranger who had led her away from the crowd.

There was writing on the paper. It was hard to make it out, but finally, she deciphered it. In a fancy script it read, "Go to the Mosque; find the answers to your questions."

Millie stood under the street light trying to figure out what she should do. Was this a general advertisement or was it meant just for her? What mosque was the note referring to? There were hundreds of mosques in Istanbul.

Down the block, a car engine started, the headlights of a parked vehicle came on, and the vehicle slowly approached her. It was a black limousine. It pulled up in front of her and stopped.

It was an awkward moment. She was standing under a street lamp, alone, about three o'clock in the morning, on a deserted street. And a limousine with tinted windows and its motor purring had positioned itself beside her. There was a lot of room here for a misunderstanding.

Millie began limping down the boulevard in the opposite direction the limo was faced with as much dignity as she could muster.

She heard a door of the limo open and she stopped and turned back to see a chauffeur standing on the sidewalk beside the limo.

"Do you wish to go to the Mosque?" the chauffeur asked.

After a moment, Millie responded. "I really wish to go back to America!"

"I am here to take you to the Mosque." His voice was formal.

"Who sent you?" Millie asked. There was no response. "Who is your employer?"

"I cannot divulge that information, madam. I am here to take you to the Mosque if you so desire."

Millie considered the alternatives. The street in front of her was deserted. There is no telling what weirdoes or worse might be hiding there.

Whoever wanted her to go to the Mosque at least had money to send a limo to get her there. If he wanted to harm her, he didn't have to send a limo to do it. She was not far enough from the street lamp light that she could not re-read the message on the piece of paper still in her hand, "Go to the Mosque; find the answers to your questions."

She certainly had questions.

"Okay," Millie sighed. "Let's go to the Mosque and get some answers."

The chauffeur opened the rear door for her and she got into cushioned, leather luxury. The chauffeur shut the door and went around and got back into the driver's seat.

It was a very smooth, quiet ride through a sleeping city. They drove to the Asian side of the Bosporus and then along the river.

The neighborhood of the Mosque was wealth. Large forbidding buildings set on extensive, manicured grounds, fountains, and entrance gates. All illuminated by security lights. They reminded Millie of William Randolph Hearst's mansion at San Simeon.

Millie could not imagine anyone taking a puppy dog for a stroll down the block or popping out to walk to the corner grocery for a carton of milk. The whole neighborhood gave her the creeps. It was like driving through an oversized, deluxe necropolis.

The limo passed under a golden gate and approached what must be the Mosque, judging by the two slender minaret towers that flanked it and the dome centered on the square building.

When the limo came as close to the Mosque as the road permitted, the limo came to a stop and the driver came around and opened the door for Millie.

"Am I to go in there — by myself?" she asked.

The chauffeur nodded in the affirmative. His face was noncommittal. He looked to Millie to be a man who in his younger days might have been a soldier of fortune; not a native of Turkey. He had no moustache.

She started slowly toward the Mosque.

"Madam." The chauffeur had not moved. He was holding something. "Put this over your head. Out of respect."

"Sure," Millie said and took the white silk head dress he offered her, donned it and limped toward the silent dark marble building.

She had never been in a mosque, and had no idea what to expect. Beyond the large, solid doors which were open enough for her to pass there was a marble foyer. Beyond the empty foyer, a large open room. Nothing there. Dim lights from hidden sources revealed an impersonal interior. The walls were covered with abstract, multi-colored mosaics. Above was a gigantic dome with an enormous scimitar. (Cabot Cabot had said the scimitar in a mosque always pointed in the direction of Mecca.) The marble floor was decorated with geometric designs. There was nothing in the hall. It was absolute emptiness, ringed by pale stone pillars. It was quiet. It was large. It was cold.

Was this once a church that had been converted to a mosque when the Ottoman Turks rode into town in 1453 or was this a mosque built by the famous Sinan, who designed over forty mosques for Suleiman the Magnificent?

Cabot Cabot had told Mary Jo, Weinstein and Millie that there were so many beautiful structures in Istanbul that began as churches, were turned into mosques and with the demise of the Ottoman Empire became museums for the tourists.

She was about to turn and leave when a sixth sense sensation of someone else's presence came to her. She had the feeling she was being watched.

Maybe she was to say some prayers to Allah here and get the answer to all her questions. She stood just inside the large empty room wondering what to do.

She really didn't believe in any god. She had no time in her life for gods. If there was a God, He had a lot of answering to do, as far as Millie was concerned, for the senseless deaths of her husband and son. Her search for the meaning of life never included Him.

She was about to turn and leave when a voice came from behind a pillar:

"Mrs. Sharp?" It was the voice of a young woman.

Millie's back arched. She was shocked that someone

here knew her name. She stood her ground. "I am Mrs. Sharp. Who are you?"

"That is not important. What is important is you should know there are those in Istanbul who want to take your life."

"Why?!" Millie shouted.

"I want to help you get out of Istanbul," the young woman behind one of the pillars said. "There has been enough bloodshed."

"Why would anyone want to kill me?!" Millie cried

"Because you deserve to die." The young woman was stating a fact in a dispassionate tone.

Millie would have written the young lady behind the pillars off as crazy and turned and limped out, but — the shooting at the airport, the bombing of the Ottoman Grande, the mobs that had tried to tear her to pieces and the nightmare at Troy, Chalmer's dying words — Indeed, it did seem like people were out to kill her. It wasn't paranoia.

"Why do I deserve to die?! What have I done to any-one in Turkey?!" Millie cried.

There was a long pause. "You do not know?" There was surprise mixed with a contempt.

"No, I don't!" Millie cried.

"It cannot be that you do not know." The voice be-hind the pillars seemed to be moving, as if the young lady were passing from pillar to pillar, circling around Millie.

"It's true!" Millie directed her bewilderment in the direction of the voice.

"Maybe that you do not know — is why Allah has preserved you by circumstances from the attempts that have been made on your life.

"Before you die, you should know!" The young lady behind the pillars appeared to have resolved her problem.

"Know *what?!* What have I done?!" Millie tried to keep focused on where the voice was moving. She dared not run to the voice. The young woman might decide to put a bullet in her and get the killing over without any further proceedings.

"You have caused the greatest sorrow to a family. *A family that has the resources to avenge.*

"Does the name Rashid Havabaddaddie mean nothing to you?!" The voice had made almost a full circle and was at the pillars closest to the entrance to the large room. If Millie attempted to run, the young woman could easily step out and block her way.

". . . Who is Rashid Hava...what?!" Millie was completely at a loss. "And what did I do to him?"

"It is not true that you do not know Rashid Havabaddaddie! You are responsible for his death!" The young woman was angry.

"You have the wrong person! I don't know who you're talking about!" Millie cried.

"There is a room reserved for you. The chauffeur will take you there. It is a small respectful hotel." The young woman behind the pillars regained her composure.

"A message will come to you when the boat is ready to receive you to take you away to safety in Greece.

"You can choose not to go to the hotel. You can choose not to take the boat to safety in Greece. You can walk away, and those who seek revenge will surely hunt you down and kill you —no matter wherever you go. And they will also kill all your miserable friends that came to Istanbul with you.

Their fate and your own is in your hands.

"Go to the hotel, catch the boat when it is ready for you and I will arrange that your friends will be spared." The young woman's voice seemed to be receding.

"Who are you?" Millie asked.

No answer came. Millie waited. And waited.

"Hello? Are you there?" Millie slowly approached the pillars. The other side was in darkness.

After a few more moments, Millie realized she was alone. She turned and left the Mosque.

The chauffeur was standing by the limo. He opened the door as she approached.

CHAPTER 11

"We see things not as they are, but as we are."
— Talmud

*P*erhaps she should not have gone to the small hotel where a room was reserved for her.

But what was the alternative?

It was about four a.m. when she left the Mosque. If she limped away, where could she go? How would she get there? How far would she get in this neighborhood on foot? Within minutes she would be in the hands of the police.

Moreover, she was exhausted. A room in a small hotel was exactly what she wanted. She had not had any real sleep in almost two days — since they left Izzy's place. . . and her stomach was beginning to churn from too many pastries and raki at the Comfort Zone.

She didn't want to think about Izzy, or Chalmers, or what might have happened to O'Brien, Weinstein and Fowler and the others. And why someone would want to kill her because of . . . "Rashid Hava-whatever"?! Who the hell was Rashid Hava. . .?! She couldn't remember what the last name was. She was certain she had never heard it before tonight.

Before arriving in Istanbul, life had lost all meaning. Now, life was turning absolutely insane. And forget the luxury of "meaning," the only game was survival.

She just craved sleep! She could hardly keep her eyes open. Maybe it would be good if someone killed her; she could get some sleep.

And so she let the chauffeur drive her to the small

hotel. She couldn't tell you where it was. She fell asleep on the way. The chauffeur had to waken her and guide her to the door of the hotel.

They knew she was coming. She was taken by a porter up on an elevator to a room.

It was a very nice, clean room with floral wallpaper. Any room with or without floral wallpaper would have been nice. The porter left her and she collapsed on the bed and was asleep immediately.

***

The sun was shining and there was a soft knock on the door that awoke her. She didn't want to wake up, but the knocking persisted. She mumbled.

The knocking continued louder.

"What now?" Maybe the knocking would stop if she responded.

"Do you wish something to eat or drink, madam?" came the humble voice of someone who sounded like he might be a hotel employee.

She thought about it. "Give me a half hour."

"What would you like, madam? I will bring it in a half hour?" the voice on the other side of the door asked.

"Tea. Buttered toast, two poached eggs. . . . And orange juice. . . And tea, did I say tea?" she added.

"Yes, madam. I bring in half of an hour," the humble voice responded.

The room came with a bath — a bath with sparking gold fixtures, white porcelain and plenty of — what else? — Turkish towels; in all different colors. And scented soaps. She picked "blue grass."

She was thinking how nice it would be to have a change of clothes, when coming out of the bathroom she received a pleasant shock — there on a chair by the bed was an outfit, including shoes and intimate wear. She was positive the clothes weren't there when she went in for a shower. This was quite a hotel! Not only did it provide breakfast to your room, but a new ensemble!

It was all silk and very feminine and cut in a style that Millie was not accustomed to. The dress seemed like it was designed by someone that couldn't make up his mind whether he was designing for the Western woman or the Eastern woman. Ruffles at the neck and waist, long sleeves and a hemline that went almost to the ankles. The dress was white and the shoes were white. And it all was a perfect fit. Whoever had arranged for the clothing knew her sizes. She was happy with how she looked in the outfit and felt like a new person when the porter came knocking at the door with breakfast on a tray.

It was a late breakfast. The porter informed her it was almost two o'clock. He did not remark on her being in new clothes. And Millie did not ask him if he knew how the clothes came to be in the room.

The porter returned an hour later to take away the breakfast tray and to give her a sealed envelope.

At first Millie thought this must be the bill for the room, breakfast and clothes.

It wasn't. In the florid handwriting of last night's note and on the same expensive linen paper that told her to go to the Mosque the note read:

"Not far from the hotel is the Haliç, (the Golden Horn) which flows into the Bosporus. Go to the Galata Kulesi docks

on the Haliç. Find Gümüpala Cad, berth no. XV. There will
be a boat there for you at six p.m.

"Precisely at six p.m. ask the captain of the boat in
berth no. XV on Gümüpala Cad if he has room for one more.
Tell him you are a friend of Rashid. Dress in the white dress.

"Do this and all will be well for you. When you are
on your way, out of the Haliç, out of the Bosporus, when you
are in the Sea of Marmara, the captain will come to you and
give you an envelope. It will contain a hundred thousand
dollars in American money and new identity papers to get
started on a new life in Greece.

"If you fail in any of these instructions, if you fail to
catch the boat, you and your friends will be dead.

"Advisable for your safety, destroy this note upon
committing to memory the essential parts."

It was unsigned.

Whoever was engineering all this really wanted her
out of Turkey and out of her being who she was.

Was it the young lady behind the Mosque pillars who
earlier this morning said she wanted to end the bloodshed?
Wanted to help her get out of Istanbul, out of Turkey and into
Greece. . . Did the lady behind the pillars arrange all this? Or
was there someone behind the lady of the Mosque?

And who was Rashid Hava— hava—? And why was
it thought that she—

Ohmygod! Ohmygod! In a flash she had a good idea
who Rashid must be!

It was her intuition that spoke to her, after a good
night's sleep, a shower and a breakfast.   Her intuition and
subconscious were back on the job.

Rashid Hava... whatever — had to be Richard Smith.

Richard Smith was the name he used in America. The name his wife knew him by when Millie filed the divorce papers on her behalf.

Attorneys in their careers handle thousands of cases. And like many attorneys, Millie often forgot the names of most. Generally, names were just buried in files. But some of the stories she would never forget.

The story of *Stella Smith v. Richard Smith* was one of the stories she would never forget. It was a divorce case with a very bitter child custody battle.

There were allegations made by Stella that Richard had beat her and their two minor children. Richard denied the charge.

Whatever the truth was, the court awarded Stella custody of the two children.

Secretly, Millie always suspected the court's decision might have had more to do with her legal skills and the deficiencies of Richard's attorney, than with the facts. No criminal charges were ever filed against Richard. But an attorney does not voice to the court her suspicions about her client's allegations. That's not playing the game.

The court awarded Stella the children and that was all Stella wanted, and Millie was working for Stella, not for some "truth," Millie told herself.

Millie tried to get Stella to be liberal about visitation. But Stella didn't want to give Richard any visitation.

Then things turned ugly. Stella alleged Richard attempted to kidnap the children and leave the country.

The court's response was to deny Richard all visitation rights. And the police started looking into the allegation of kidnaping. Then abruptly, the battle ended. Richard committed suicide.

What was not strictly relevant to the divorce proceedings, became important to Millie now. Richard's last name was not really "Smith." Everyone knew that from the start. It really didn't matter in the divorce proceedings that he was an "undocumented" (i.e. illegal) alien from an unspecified country. His legal status was not relevant to the divorce.

Stella knew next to nothing about Richard's family. Richard told Stella his family were bad people; it would be best to forget them. And that is exactly what they did.

Over the course of many hours in Millie's office, Millie heard the details. Stella's and Richard's two children drew pictures in coloring books, as Millie and Stella discussed the case.

Rashid had to be Richard.

Millie left her room and went down to the hotel lobby. With the assistance of the same man who brought her breakfast, she made several phone calls — to the American Embassy, to the American Consulate office in Istanbul, to the Warehouse Hotel. The Embassy and the Consulate both had a recording telling her to leave a message and they would get back to her as soon as possible. At the Warehouse Hotel, she was told none of her friends were there. They had all left.

She asked the humble man who brought her the breakfast and helped her with the phone calling and seemed to be running the hotel with no guests but herself, many questions. Like, who was paying for her staying there? How did the clothes she was wearing get in her room? Had he ever heard of a Rashid Hava... something.

She got nowhere. He could give her no answers. Only smiles and shrugs and he would ask if she wanted anything else to eat. Perhaps, some oranges and sliced apples or some more tea. He recommended the apple tea, Turkey's favorite.

Millie declined all offers of food and drink. It was almost four o'clock by the grandfather clock in the lobby. It was time to face the world and find a boat.

"Can you tell me which direction to go for the Golden Horn?" she asked the porter.

He smiled, nodded. Finally, he could answer a question. He led her out on to the street and pointed her in the right direction.

CHAPTER 12

"Miracles seem to rest, not so much upon faces or voices
or healing power coming suddenly near to us from far off,
but upon our perceptions being made finer so that for a
moment our eyes can see and our ears can hear
that which is about us always."
— Willa Cather

$\mathcal{F}$ inding the Golden Horn came easier than she thought. It was a straight six block walk from the hotel.

On the walk she passed many beautiful buildings, no doubt each with a history running back hundreds, and more likely thousands of years. And many shops she would have liked to have spent some time in.

She regretted that she did not have time to see any of the great sights of Istanbul — that Cabot Cabot would, no doubt, have taken them to if things had been different.

Sights like St. Sofia, the Church of the Divine Wisdom with its "sweating column" believed to cure illnesses. Built in 537 A.D. by the Emperor Justinian to rival Solomon's Temple in grandeur, St. Sofia, like all the other Byzantium churches, was quickly converted to a mosque when Constaninople became Instanbul in 1453.

When the Atatürk and the secularists took power, in the 1920's, St. Sophia became a museum, a tourist attraction.

She would have liked to have visited the Topkapi palace, home for Sultans and their harems for hundreds of years. Now another museum — enshrining Ottoman opulence as a butterfly stuck thru with a pin on black velvet enshrines butterfly beauty, but is no longer the butterfly.

And she never got to buy a Turkish carpet.

Oh, well! You can't have everything. She should be thankful she was getting out of Turkey with her life.

Here was the Golden Horn and the Gümüpala Cad, which appeared to be the road running along the Golden Horn waterway. There were vendors of all sorts along the Gümüpala Cad and many tourists. Quite a busy walkway. Reminded Millie a little of the Boardwalk in Atlantic City.

Now to find Kulesi docks, berth number XV, recalling the 'essential parts' of the note she received at the hotel.

It didn't take long. There was a line of small boats, hundreds of them. And a sign that read, "Kulesi docks."

And there was berth number XV, and there was a very weather-beaten old skiff. It couldn't have been more than thirty feet long. There was a raised cabin in the center. It looked like it had been once painted white, but that must have been about fifty years ago.

It was not quite five. She was to present herself at the boat in berth number XV precisely at six. She could stand and wait till six, staring at the boat or she could get her last mini-tour of Istanbul.

She decided to turn back on the street she had just come down and stop in a shop she passed that had Turkish carpets in the window. Maybe she just might be able to get herself a small carpet before she left.

Walking back she couldn't find the shop. Had it shut up early? Shops that closed seemed to go into a shell and you couldn't tell where they were because all they presented to the world closed was the crenelated metal shell.

Time was growing short. Well, if she couldn't find

the shop, there was at least the beautiful building that had caught her eye. No one could hide it with a crenelated metal shell. She was drawn to the building and curious to see what was inside.

Inside, she discovered quickly enough that it was a church. She felt a little awkward. She turned to leave, but the next instant turned back and looked at the very elaborate, overwhelming beauty of the church's altar.

She stared at the altar. It evoked memories of her grandmother. Her grandmother was a devout Christian, whom Millie did not get to see much of — because she was a devout Christian.

Millie's mother thought her mother (Millie's grandmother) was a religious fanatic and Millie's mother didn't want Millie infected with the old woman's superstitious rubbish. Millie recalled a Biblical verse her grandmother had repeated to her over and over— "Call on to me and I will answer thee and show thee great and marvelous things thou knowest not." Her grandmother told her to never forget it, — that, "You can call on God and He will always answer your prayers."

Her grandmother told her that prayer never failed her.

Millie didn't see much of her grandmother. Millie's mother told Millie her grandmother wasn't right in her head.

Millie's mother raised Millie to think for herself and rely only on her own thinking.

Maybe her mother was right, but when you can't solve a problem, it would be nice to have someone to turn to for help.

Kneeling in one of the pews, Millie said a quiet prayer to the God she didn't believe in. She also added, "Grandma, if you're listening. . . Talk to Him for me, will you?"

Outside, in the real world, nothing had changed. She had no answers. Still, she had to admit to herself she felt an odd sensation of peace. Guess that's what keeps churches going, she thought — it gives people a sense of peace of mind. Cheaper than a pill, and maybe less side-effects. Immediately, she could hear her mother saying, The Inquisition was a hell of a side-effect.

Quietly, she walked back to the Golden Horn to be ready precisely at six to approach the old skiff in berth XV.

There was a sidewalk cafe not too far from berth XV. Millie thought she would have a bite to eat before boarding. It was a little after five.

She ordered a fish sandwich and tea. Apple tea, Turkey's favorite. And she thought of the children of Stella and Richard. How they wanted to see their father, and go with him to see their grandfather.

Millie wished she had the time to find the grandfather and tell him the children wanted to see him. And perhaps she could help the grandfather get to see them. But it would be impossible to find him.

Catching the boat was the logical thing. Forget a quixotic attempt to find Rashid's father.

The waiter brought the fish sandwich and tea.

From where she sat on the water side of the Gümüpala Cad, she could observe the skiff, where she would present herself at precisely at six p.m.

And then it began to happen.

There must be a word for what happened. Millie could not put a word on it. Or if she could put a word on it, the word was not allowed into her frame of reality. In psychol-

ogy, they might call it synchronicity. In fiction, contrivance.
To some religious people, it might be a miracle. To most of
us it was just an odd sequence of events, which, if we are
honest with ourselves, we have all experienced at one time or
another.

She couldn't explain it, she could only recount the
sequence of events. Each event in itself being trivial, but in
sequence it lead to the monumental.

It was silly. It was so trivial how the sequence began.
But this is what happened:

A stray cat stood at her feet and watched her eating
her fish sandwich. No doubt, the cat was waiting for her to
give him a piece of the sandwich.

Across from the bistro, on the landside of the road
was a series of shops. One shop directly across from where
she sat caught her attention. It was was boarded up. Boarded
up not for the night, but in the way of abandoned buildings.
Plywood covered the entrance and windows. A faded sign
on the shop read something in various languages.

What particularly caught Millie's curiosity was while
she sat and ate her fish sandwich, in the span of several minutes, three well-polished motor vehicles pulled up in front of
the boarded up shop.

In each case, someone got out of the rear passenger
side, and the expensive car drove away.

Each of the men dropped outside the boarded up shop
appeared to be a carbon copy of the first in dress and actions.
Each wore a dark suit and black tie. Each looked left and
right and then disappeared down an alley that ran on the
northside of the boarded building.

On the northside of the boarded building, the other

side of the alley, was a bookshop with stocked bookracks outside the shop, which suggested the shop was still open. Millie thought of going over there after she finished her sandwich.

Why were the men going down the alley? she wondered. Could they all be entering a rear door of the bookstore?

Millie idly wondered who the men might be and what they would be doing going down the alley that ran on the northside of the boarded up shop.

And then out of the blue, for no logical reason another thought popped into her head. She remembered Richard's (Rashid's) children in her office with their mother. They were drawing pictures with crayons.

The little boy —Arie — had said something about his grandfather "hid with cats." And his sister, Helena, responded, "And he has lots of combs for the cats."

The children giggled and crayoned. It was just silly childish nonsense talk at the time with no meaning.

Why did it pop into Millie's head now? Any incident from the past, however trivial, can unannounced come crashing into our present thoughts, sort of like a book falling off a shelf.

Then Millie read the sign on the boarded up building: "Istanbul's Catacombs." The little boy said his grandfather "hid with the cats," and his sister replied, "And he has lots of combs for the cats." It may have been childish nonsense, but was it based on something their father (Richard/Rashid) had said to them?

Millie put down the remainder of the fish sandwich in front of the patient cat at her feet. And, as if in an hypnotic dream, she crossed the street to the deserted building.

She stared at the building and whispered to herself, "Now what?"

The front door had a big padlock on it, and a faded official document nailed to the door. The document was not in English but in the same alphabet. Cabot Cabot had told them that Atatürk had abolished the Arabic alphabet for the Turkish language. Millie guessed this must be a Turkish government notice of some kind.

And then the name popped up out of the writing. "Havabaddaddie." She recognized it immediately. That was the name given as Rashid's last name by the lady of the Mosque.

She walked to the north side of the building.   The alley the men had gone down. It was an alley filled with trash. She took a tentative step into the alley.

And another and another. Halfway down the alley there was a side door.

And it was open by just a crack.

No rational person would enter a side door in a deserted building. But Millie wasn't being guided by reason at this point. There was something else in control of her actions.

She pushed the door in. Nothing could be seen on the inside.

In her purse she had a very small flashlight attached to a key ring. Schwietz had given it to her as a promotional item years ago when he was running for some office. Every once and in a while, Millie found the small flashlight handy. This was one time.

Inside, there was a narrow hall leading toward the back

of the building. She walked along slowly and quietly.

At the end of the hall. There was another hall that looked like it might run to the other side of the building. She turned around to leave and found someone blocking her way.

CHAPTER 13

"Will you walk into my Parlor?"
said the Spider to the Fly;
"Tis the prettiest little parlor
that ever you did spy."
— Mary Howitt
'The Spider and the Fly' (1844)

*S*he couldn't see very well in the dark, but her penlight revealed the man blocking her way had a gun pointed at her. He motioned her to turn around and walk down the hallway she had turned away from. As much as Millie loathe guns, she had to concede they were persuasive.

They proceeded down the hallway. At the midway point to the other side of the building, there was a door. Her escort knocked.

Someone on the other side opened. And Millie and the man with the gun stepped into a well-lit, well-decorated conference room, a big contrast from the deserted appearance of the building's exterior.

All the men that Millie had seen earlier dropped off by polished cars were here, plus others. They all looked up in surprise when Millie entered. More than surprise — Resentment. She was crashing their private party.

So many of them had beards and were dressed in black, it looked like a Turkish version of Rembrandt's "Old Dutch Masters," featured on her grandfather's cigar boxes.

The old Turkish Masters turned to the man at the head of the table for guidance. He stood and said something to them, presumably in Turkish.

The Old Masters stood and left the room. They went out another door that would put them further into the building. It was clear from their looks they didn't like Millie interrupting. As if she had disrupted a board of directors meeting to bring silly domestic matter to the attention of the chairman.

There remained in the room only the man with the gun. The man at the head of the table gave him an instruction, presumably in Turkish, and the man and his gun went back into the hallway, closing the door.

It was Millie and the man at the head of the table alone in the conference room.

She recognized him immediately. He was the Omar Sharif look-a-like that she saw at the Whirling Dervish and the Golden Ramekin. At the Golden Ramekin their eyes had locked in recognition, and Millie was mesmerized as Cabot Cabot was having a heart attack.

Nothing was said for a full moment.

Was she experiencing the magic of Istanbul that Bob Bohnert had spoken of? Was meaning flowing back into her life?

"Please have a seat, Mrs. Sharp," he said.

She gave no answer, but she sat at the table and wondered how he knew her name.

"Would you care for something to drink?" he said. His voice was as soft as butter; his manner as gentle as silk.

He took up a bottle and two glasses from a sidebar and came and sat by her and poured wine into the glasses.

Millie stared in wonder. She could think of nothing to say.

He raised his glass. *"Pour vous."* It was almost a whisper. He took a sip of his drink, put it down and took out a pack of Turkish cigarettes. He offered her one.

She shook her head in the negative. She never liked cigarette smoke. But if he smoked she wouldn't mind.

He took out a lighter and lit a thin black cigarette, that gave off the pleasant aroma of licorice.

His movements were slow and deliberate. Millie had the feeling she was in the presence of the most refined, most intelligent, most sensitive man in existence.

They stared at each other for several more moments.

And finally, he spoke. "You absolutely amaze me, Mrs. Sharp."

The feeling was mutual, but Millie wasn't going to tell him. He could read it in her face.

"Who are you?" she asked almost matching his tone. "You know my name, but I don't who you are."

"Who I am is of no consequence," he said. "Who you are is."

"Are you Mr. Hava— Havabaddaddie?" she asked, proud of herself that she remembered the whole name. "Are you the father of Rashid Havabaddaddie who went to America and changed his name to Richard Smith?"

"No," he said, and almost smiled.

"Oh. Then, who are you? And where is Mr. Havabaddaddie — his name is on the notice on the door." Millie looked around the room as if Mr. Havabaddaddie might be hiding behind one of the Greek statutes that decorated the room.

"Mr. Havabaddaddie was an associate of mine. His son, Rashid, did go to America and change his name."

"To Richard Smith," Millie contributed.

"Mr. Havabaddaddie was quite devastated. His son had turned his back on his country, his heritage, his family, and chose to become an American.

"When Rashid took an American wife and they never came to see the family in Istanbul, Mr. Havabaddaddie became ill.

"As you well-know, Mrs. Sharp, Rashid and his American wife separated and Rashid was denied visits with his children.

"When word came that Rashid had taken his life, my good friend and associate. . . died heartbroken."

"Oh! I'm so sorry," Millie muttered.

They stared at each other for another long moment.

Finally, Millie asked, "How did you get involved?"

He gave a slight shrug. "Mr. Havabaddaddie was, as I've said, my good friend and associate.

"He asked for my help. Mr. Havabaddaddie was a very proud man. Unfortunately, he came to me too late. After his son had committed suicide.

"There was really nothing to be done. . . He was not interested in securing his grandchildren. He had enough grandchildren and, besides, the two in America from all reports were spoiled."

"They would have very much liked to have known their grandfather," Millie interjected.

"That may have been. . . I am sorry they did not have the opportunity." He looked away for a moment and then returned his gaze into her eyes.

It was to Millie as if his gaze went to her very soul. No one had ever looked at her like this before. They stared at each other. Millie could not say how long it was before the conversation started up again. What they were talking about was important, but their eyes were carrying on their own conversation that had no words.

At long last, the intimacy of staring was too revealing. She cleared her throat and asked, "You were saying how you got involved."

He put out his cigarette and lit another. "When word came that his son committed suicide, there was nothing left for my good friend. Nothing left but — revenge."

"Revenge?" How could such an ugly word intrude on this moment, she wondered.

"Yes, against the one person most responsible for bringing his son to kill himself."

"And who was that?" she asked.

It was a long moment of staring before he answered. "You."

"Me?! I only represented his wife, who wanted a divorce, how was I responsible for his committing suicide?!" This was not the conversation she wanted to have with him.

"We secured all the court filings and tapes of the proceedings.

"It was determined by all in the family who read these legal documents and listened to the tapes that it was you who distorted reality.

"If his wife had not turned to you, if they had turned to family, instead of an attorney, they would have found peace." He said all of this calmly, dispassionately.

It was Millie who found it difficult to remain calm. "He was physically abusing her and the children!"

He stared at her for the longest time and said nothing.

"I did not make up the allegations of Stella Smith!" Millie protested. "The children were interviewed by a psychologist! They had been physically chastised by their father!"

Why was it so important that she convince him, she asked herself? She was not really sure of what the truth was. She only knew what the evidence was. She stopped speaking, sensing her words were hollow and she was not convincing him of anything. "We have different standards of what is abuse in America." Her voice trailed off.

There was a long moment of silence.

Finally, he said softly, "Yes, we come from different cultures, Mrs. Sharp."

"Rashid came to America. He wanted to be an American. If so, he had to abide by our laws. I did not make anything up! I did not put words in Mrs. Sharp's mouth or the children's mouths, and I am certainly not responsible for Rashid's suicide! Perhaps, if he had sought counseling. . ." Again her voice trailed off. She wanted him to understand. But there was nothing more that she could say.

They stared at each other. A timeless stare. An hypnotic stare. A stare that was a stair to another plateau of existence, an existence in a higher key, as with classical music.

"You fascinate me, Mrs. Sharp," he whispered.

If he had recited Persian poetry, she would have listened for hours.

If he had said, Move to Turkey and take up finger painting, she would asked, which fingers? And where are the paints?

If he had said, Let us run off and herd sheep on the mountain slopes of Outer Mongolia, she would only have asked, How do we get to Mongolia from here?

But, he said, instead, "You fascinate me — because you are not dead."

"What?"

"You're survivability," he said.

"My what?"

"You have managed to escape death, so many times."

She had "managed to escape death, so many times." The near plane crash over the Atlantic, the escape from the plains of Troy, the mob outside the Comfort Zone. . . How did he know of all these brushes with death?

A door opened. Inspector Jurice Kamal entered, not with drawn gun, but casually. He crossed to and whispered in the ear of the man who looked like a movie star, the man who said his name was of no consequence, the man who had just said she amazed him because she managed to escape death so many times.

They exchanged a few words in what Millie presumed to be the Turkish tongue. Was Inspector Kamal there to take her off to jail?

Inspector Kamal stood by respectfully. For a second, Millie and he made eye contact. Was she imaging that he was almost smiling?!

"As I was saying," he continued, "you amaze me. From the car crash to your declining a boat ride escape from Turkey that would only have had you fed to the fishes in the Sea of Marmara — you live a life that almost persuades me, Mrs. Sharp, that there is a guardian angel sitting on your shoulder."

She almost didn't hear it. It was said so softly, so off-handed—*"From the car crash"?* She repeated it in a whisper.

"Yes," he said. "The death of your husband and son—" He sighed. "The matter should have dropped there. It was some in the family who would not let it end there. They wanted *your* life."

"*You* were responsible for my husband and son's death?" The question came from deep inside her.

"We did not intend them. It was your car. It was *you* we wanted."

They stared at each.

What was she looking at? A man she was overwhelmingly attracted to *and* a man who was the monster responsible for the death of her husband and her son. In an odd way, she told herself, she was looking at the universe —a universe of beauty *and* ugliness, good *and* evil, joy *and* suffering, love *and* hate, rapture *and* cold indifference.

He took a small revolver out of an inside jacket pocket and placed it on the table between them.

"I say we are even," he whispered. "Go in peace, Mrs. Sharp. You have my word — you will be safely returned to your country and no one — no one— will ever bother you again. I will see to it."

Millie looked at the gun and glanced up at Inspector Kamal. His eyes moved from the gun to Millie. He nodded slightly, as if in agreement with . . .the man who was responsible for the deaths of her husband and son.

"What do you say, Mrs. Sharp?"

For a second Millie looked away and then turned back, and swiftly took the gun off the table and shot the man who killed her husband and son.

She shot him in the chest. In the heart. With what appeared to Millie as an enigmatic smile on his face —and love in his eyes!!—his head collapsed on to his chest and his body remained in the chair. It was as if he just fell asleep.

She immediately turned the gun on Inspector Kamal who was already reaching for his holstered gun. He stopped reaching and stood at attention.

"Congratulations, madam," Kamal said. "You have just shot Turkey's public enemy number one. You have killed the Spider!"

She kept the gun pointed at Kamal.

"I will see you safely out of the country. You will not want to stay around for the legal inquiries, which can be lengthy and tiresome. I will protect you from all that. I guarantee your safe passage," he said.

"Like you did the people of Lypii?" she said.

He got a panicky look on his face. "I assure you—"

She shot him in the chest. "For Maslova!"

He fell immediately to the floor.

She stood up, dropped the gun, turned and walked out the door she came in.

She expected to be stopped by the 500 pounds of meat that had brought her into the room. He wasn't there. She didn't really think about where he might be. In a daze, she slowly walked out of the building and down the street.

No one stopped her.

At first she didn't know where she was going or even care. Then she decided to return to the church she had said a prayer in earlier. She wanted a prayer in the church before they arrested her.

A truck pulled up along side her. There were four men in it.

"Mrs. Sharp?" one of the men said.

"Yes," she said, not afraid of admitting who she was. Not really caring what happened.

"Please, get in."

CHAPTER 14

Peace I leave with you; my peace I give unto you:
not as the world giveth, give I unto you.
Let not your heart be troubled, neither let it be afraid.
                                        — John 14:26-28

*M*illie opened her eyes and Weinstein was seated beside her on her right side, and O'Brien was seated on her left. For a second she thought, Oh no, they have them, too!

Then, she realized there was an armrest on both sides of her and they were sitting in comfortable seats in a large airplane.

Was this a dream? No, it wasn't a dream. Slowly it began coming back to her.

The four men in the truck that picked her up were Americans. Special forces. They drove her to an American air base. She was rushed onto the plane and here they were in the air.

O'Brien and Weinstein had filled her in. She was given a sedative by the stewardess and she drifted off.

It all came back now.

The man across the aisle with his face and most of his body wrapped in bandages was John Fowler.

O'Brien and Weinstein told her how Fowler was in Turkey on a military mission to train a special kind of dog, a Turkey mountain shih tzu, (a breed found only in Turkey) to dance. (What military value dancing dogs would have was not/could not be revealed.) It was these dogs that were dancing that distracted the mob when they left the Comfort Zone.

Something had gone wrong, though. The mob, the dogs, the music abruptly stopping— and in the melee, Fowler was attacked by his dogs.

"He still loves all dogs," said Weinstein, "except for a certain Turkish mountain breed which are lousy dancers."

Someone was sneezing and coughing a few seats in front of them. "That's Casey McCall," Weinstein explained. "He caught pneumonia swimming the Hellespont. But on the third try he did get across before they caught him! And despite the pneumonia, he's got a big smile on his face."

"Why did he do it?!" Millie asked.

"Well, he won't say, but the best we can figure is Casey has always lived in the shadow of his dad. His dad, as you know, was a great attorney —but his dad never swam the Hellespont," O'Brien explained.

"I don't get it," Millie said.

"He's come out from under the shadow. He's done one thing, his dad never did," Weinstein elaborated. "And probably never will do."

Millie still didn't understand it, but had to accept it.

Someone several seats ahead was crying and every once in a while would give out a loud moan.

"That's J.R. He's had a rough time of it," Weinstein said.

"They gave him a big blue—" O'Brien said.

"Pill?!" Millie asked.

"Yes, medication. But it seems to have had negative consequences. J.R.'s always been a bundle of sensitivity to allergic reactions, but this! The big blue made his arms, hands and legs turn blue and itch all over."

"And the nightmares!" Weinstein added.

"Nightmares?" Millie asked.

"Yeah. He's had some real pips!" O'Brien said. "Like losing money, and having no good suits to wear."

"The worst was the dream in which he was taking an anger management class taught by Séan Doyle!" Weinstein winced at the thought. [Ed. Note: The best scholarly research suggests that Séan Doyle teaching an anger management class was comparable to Attila the Hun teaching etiquette. See *Revolt of the Doyle Clerks,* Number 13 in the TALES OF THE HALL series.]

"Oh, God, forgive us all our ignorance! Bring us all to repent! Show all mankind, which incidentally I love, God —You know I love all mankind! — Show them that life is short, very short—" A moaning, crying, nose blowing and sniffing momentarily interrupted the flow of shouted words — "And we should all . . .we should all . . . do . . .do what we can. . . for . . .for each other!. . . Oh, Steve! Steve, where art thou?! Forgive me, Steve! Forgive me!" It was the voice of J.R. crying in the wilderness. Or more precise, crying out a few seats up the aisle from Millie, O'Brien and Weinstein.

"Has he lost his mind?" Millie asked.

"I don't think so" Weinstein said. "The death of Esselman may have driven him temporarily over the edge, but he'll snap back."

"Esselman is dead?!" Millie said softly. "I thought he was recovering!"

"Things can happen quickly, a reversal of medical fortunes." O'Brien shook his head. "One moment you're on your way to recovery; the next moment on the way to the morgue."

"It's hard to believe. He didn't appear to have much life in him, but he was so gentle a person, and a great dancer! I almost want to join J.R. in weeping over his passing. Is the body . . . on the plane? There's sure to be a funeral service in River City." Millie was almost brought to tears.

"I don't think so," said O'Brien.

"I'm sure there will be," said Millie.

"Millie, Esselman is okay. He caught a flight out yesterday. He had cases to cover," said Weinstein.

"Cover cases? You just said he's dead! You can't cover cases when you're dead. Not even Esselman!" cried Millie. She turned to O'Brien. "Why did you say he's dead?"

O'Brien smiled. "So I lied; sue me."

"Well, why haven't you told J.R.?!"

O'Brien and Weinstein looked at each other sheepishly. "We're kind of enjoying his religious kick," O'Brien said.

"It's been a bit profitable, too," added Weinstein. "J.R. gave away all his money to us an hour ago, saying it was all dross, worthless in the next world."

"We're planning to tell him," O'Brien sighed, "as soon as the effects of the medication wear off."

"Is Mary Jo on the plane?" Millie asked.

"She stayed behind to help Cabot Cabot recuperate," Weinstein said. "He's out of the hospital and resting up on a little horse farm he has outside Istanbul. Michaels and Howard will be covering Mary Jo's cases till she gets back... whenever that may be."

Over the plane intercom, came the voice of Tom Schwietz, "Geez, I've never flown one of these babies before. It's smooth handling though. What's this button for?"

"No, no, Tom! Don't touch that one!" cried a panicky voice.

The stewardess flew past them headed for the pilot's compartment.

For an instant the lights went out and the plane engines could not be heard, and then lights and engines were back on.

The stewardess entered the pilot's compartment and there were no more voices heard from the speakers.

"He really shouldn't be at the controls, should he?" Millie said.

"Trouble is he's a hero. All the pilots find it hard to refuse him. Bringing in that Junker was no small feat," O'Brien said.

"He's going to be featured in next month's issue of *Keeping Old War Planes in the Air*," Weinstein added.

After a few minutes, Millie asked, "You guys seem to know everything; fill me in on Art Chalmers."

"We don't know everything," O'Brien said.

"What was he doing on the plains of Troy?! Who were the people that killed him? You must know something! He told me to go to the Comfort Zone and warn the 'others.' I went and found you two. He knew you'd be there. How could he know that? And why did he apologize for getting me to come to Turkey?! I had the feeling he was apologizing for setting me up. Was I set up?"

"Millie," O'Brien said softly, "the less you know, the better."

"Don't give me that crap!" She was shouting as loud as the wailing J.R., "I want to know!" She almost kicked O'Brien in the ankle. "And no more jokes!"

"She's entitled to know what role she played," said Weinstein.

"To know and forget," said O'Brien. "And never mention it to anyone because none of it happened."

And so O'Brien and Weinstein told her "what role she played":

For years, from the vantage of the only city in the world that sits on two continents, the Spider grew in power, wealth and influence as his criminal empire fed on the drug trade, smuggling of illegal aliens and procuring weapons for terrorists. Through bribes and terror he was slowly strangling Istanbul. He even brought over to his side the best the Turkish government could send against him, the "hero" of Lypii, General Jurice Kamal.

As mighty as the Spider was, paradoxically, no one seemed to know *who* he was. The best detectives in the world could not pinpoint who he was.

It was only when two River City detectives, ("Lance" Manion and Claude Ball), became curious about the break failure on Millie's car and began wondering where "Richard Smith" might be from when investigating the kidnapping charges—that a lead opened.

Then came Art Chalmers and his Istanbul CLE. Without going into details, Weinstein and O'Brien told Millie it was an educated guess that Chalmers was bribed to get her to sign up for the Istanbul CLE. And the Spider was behind it.

The FBI, the CIA, and several other deep cover agencies became very interested. "You were the bait, Millie. They weren't sure of the details, but they were hoping it was the Spider who for whatever reason wanted you in Istanbul,"

O'Brien said. "And when the Spider came for you, they would get him."

Why did the Spider want Millie in Istanbul? The best conjecture they had was the Spider wanted her in Istanbul to kill her himself in revenge for the death of his son, Rashid Havabaddaddie, a/k/a "Richard Smith."

So, the Spider was Havabaddaddie.

"But Art? Bribed?! Did he know what he was doing?!" Millie couldn't believe it. She had known Art for years. How could he? She had thought maybe he wanted to get her to go on the CLE because he had a romantic interest in her. But instead he just sold her out!

"I'd like to think he was in over his head," said Weinstein. "Didn't realize what he was doing. I'd like to think he was told to get you over to Turkey, maybe as a gag. But we'll never know. Whatever arrangement was made between him and the Spider's intermediaries died on the plains of Troy."

"They suspect it wasn't money that motivated him, but the possibility of getting the 'sword of Achilles' that was going to be handed over to him at Troy. It's turns out, Art was a Homeric fanatic," O'Brien said.

"A Homeric fanatic?" Millie echoed.

"Who would have suspected it," sighed Weinstein. "You never know about people!"

"And there's no cure for it yet," O'Brien said, shaking his head. "Though, I hear they're working on a pill for it."

Mille wanted to say, "I'm a Homeric fanatic, too! And I'll be damned if I ever take a pill to get cured!" But you have to be careful what you say to people. They might take it as a sign of anti-social behavior if she said something like that. Instead, she turned the focus to them:

"And you two? How do you know all this?" Millie asked.

"We're not at liberty to say, Millie. We just can't tell you that one," said O'Brien. And before she could respond, he brought out his ukulele and began tuning it.

She turned to Weinstein for an answer and he turned to a magazine article on "How to make a helicopter in your basement out of a washing machine."

In the seats directly in front, Larry Simon said to someone, "It was quite a CLE, wasn't it?"

To which, Millie distinctly heard someone else respond in an almost trance-like voice, "Yes, it was."

Curious to see who said "Yes it was," Millie leaned forward and saw Robert Render seated beside Simon.

Millie sat back in her seat and looked at O'Brien and Weinstein. "He can speak! He can speak!" She whispered.

"Yes, we've discovered that," Weinstein said. "Sitting next to Simon has brought him out. He hasn't said much, but he can speak."

Millie leaned forward and took another peak at Simon and Render. Simon was collating pages and saying something about all the notes he had on Professor Hafaaz's lecture:

" 'Over-population, economic chaos and disfunction — in a single nation — are conditions leading to world government.' " Simon read from his notes. "What a brilliant observation that was, don't you think?"

"Disfunction, yes," said Render, nodding his head. His

fingers tapping the square box in his lap.

Millie sat back in her seat and looked again at O'Brien and Weinstein. "What's with that little box he's always carrying?!" she whispered.

"Nobody knows." Weinstein shrugged.

"You guys seem to know everything about everyone and you don't know anything about Render seated right in front of you?!'

"On the map of human existence, he's a blank," Weinstein said.

"Speaking of boxes," O'Brien said, "I've got one for you."

"What?" Millie turned to see O'Brien producing from somewhere a package he put in her lap. "What is this?"

"Best way to find out is to open it." O'Brien was smiling.

And so she did. And took out the most beautiful Turkish carpet with intricate patterns of rich red, yellow and green threads. "How did you —?!" she almost cried. She hadn't told anyone about her desire to get a Turkish carpet.

"It wasn't me. It was those two actors you talked to at the Comfort Zone, Mary Krause and R. J. Atkinson."

And the card in the box confirmed it. "Thank you for giving two actors the best of applause —remembering our performances!" Signed: Mary K and R. J.

How did they know?! Did she get so drunk at the Comfort Zone that she blurted out she wanted a Turkish carpet? Or was it just a coincidence? Or maybe an instance of telepathic communication.

O'Brien returned to quietly strumming his ukulele and Weinstein to reading his article on making a helicopter in your basement.

Millie sat silently trying to digest it all. Fowler in his bandages working to teach dogs to dance for the military; McCall content with pneumonia for victory over the Hellespont. J.R.'s conversion; Esselman surviving being shot; Mary finding love; Schwietz landing the burning Junker at Casablanca. Render speaking! And Art Chalmers, seduced by the sword of Achilles, working up the Istanbul CLE just to get her into the Spider's web! O'Brien and Weinstein, always known to her as two libertarians, somehow working for the government!

Simon was right: It was quite a CLE!

Another question occurred to her: "Weinstein," she said.

"What?" He looked up from his article.

"You thought the shooter at the airport was trying to shoot you because he said "Ferrari" and you once had a case with a Ferrari in it. Are you still worried about him coming after you?"

"No," Weinstein said and returned to his article.

"Why not?" she asked.

"Because we've figured out he wasn't shooting at me, he was shooting at you," Weinstein said.

"Oh... What?!!" she cried. "I never had a case with a Ferrari in it!"

"We figured it out —he wasn't shouting 'Ferrari,' he was shouting 'For Arie!'"

"For Arie? Who is Arie?"

"Arie was Richard Smith's/Rashid's nickname. The shooter was a good friend of Rashid's," Weinstein said.

Of course! His son was little Arie. Sometimes the

pieces don't fall into place right away. To Weinstein, she said, "So he could still be coming after me someday."

"Not him. He was found floating in the Sea of Marmara. His throat cut," Weinstein said.

"Good God! Who—?!"

"Can only guess. Perhaps, he stepped out of line with the Spider's designs." Weinstein returned to his magazine article.

Millie sat silent.

And then it came back to her. It was always there, but they must have given her something to momentarily block it out: *She had killed two people.* Yes, it was quite a CLE!

She began weeping, clutching her Turkish carpet.

"It's okay, Millie. If you hadn't done it, those four guys in the SUV would have gone in and done it," whispered Weinstein to her.

"You want another forget-me pill?" Weinstein asked.

"No," Millie said. "I'll be all right. I don't want any more pills. Ever again. Whatever comes; whatever pain, I'm going to take it without pills."

"There are a lot people, who can't step forward, that would like to thank you, Millie. But they can't and they never will be able to — because officially it never happened. Remember — forget it. What happened, never happened. You talk about it to anyone and they'll be carting you off to an asylum." O'Brien put down his ukulele and took out his pocket flask. He offered Millie a drink.

"No thanks," Millie said. "What is it?"

"Raki, what else is there?"

Millie made a face.

"Hey, you have your carpet, I've got the national drink.

To each his own." O'Brien said, took a big swig, and resumed his strumming on his ukulele.

Weinstein was back to reading his magazine article on making a helicopter.

Millie sat silently struggling to sort out her feelings, and thought of many things:

Of Special Inspector Jurice Kamal. The "butcher of Lypii" Cabot Cabot called him. She thought of a young lady she never met: Maslova, the attractive young lady that Izzy said had half her face burnt off the night she witnessed Kamal and his men rape her mother and sisters and put a spike through her father's head.

She thought of Art, "a Homeric fanatic." Who would have ever guessed it! Poor Art, seduced by the "sword of Achilles," to get her to Istanbul! And in the end, double-crossed by the Spider.

And brave Izzy, who fought for his country, killed by the same gangsters.

She thought of all the misery the Spider brought into the world through his drug trafficking. Of the people who died in the Ottoman Grande. And, how many other people he must have murdered.

Still . . . the individual should not take the law into his own hands. In shooting the Spider and Kamal, did she not make herself as guilty as they were?

Her grandmother would have reminded her the Bible says: Vengeance is mine, saith the Lord. Her mother, like Millie herself, was a pacifist, who didn't believe in any killing. As individuals we are to forgive and love our enemies. It is for governments to deal with people like the Spider and

Kamal. And yet, O'Brien and Weinstein were suggesting the government never would have dealt with the Spider or Kamal.

She was wrong, though, no matter what anyone might say to the contrary. Like Lady McBeth, she would never be able to wash the blood off her hands. All she could do was ask a God she didn't believe in for forgiveness.

What particularly haunted her was the Spider's putting down the gun on the table. His way of offering peace between them. Why had he done that?! Surely he knew she might grab it up. It seemed both of them in one moment had acted out of character. Or reversal of character — Her "character" entered him and he put down the gun and his "character" entered her and she took up the gun.

Her intuition spoke to her and said: Millie, dear, what happened went beyond what mere words or human understanding can comprehend.

True, Millie replied to her intuition. But I'd like to think in another time and place — we could have loved each other. When he put down the gun, it was his way of acknowledging that.

Millie put her head back and shut her eyes.

It seemed like only moments later, O'Brien was tapping on her arm.

She opened her eyes. O'Brien was pointing out the window. Her first thought was: Oh no, not another wing on fire. She leaned over and saw what O'Brien was looking at: One of the most beautiful sights in the world: the Statue of Liberty.

"The Athenians had their 60 foot statute of Athena in the Parthenon. We have our Miss Liberty," Weinstein said.

It seemed like everyone on the plane was paying a silent moment of homage.

"What was it Reagan said? America is the world's last great hope," O'Brien muttered.

"Ladies and gentlemen, please buckle your seat belts. We will be landing at Kennedy within the hour."

Millie thought of all the refugees they encountered at Kennedy Airport and were sure to encounter a new wave when they landed. She felt a compassion for them. If they had time between planes, she would go and welcome some of them to America.

The U. S. was, indeed, a lifeboat in a crazy world.

What was so special about the U. S.? Was it the equality? The freedom? Or just the welfare goodies?

Would the large numbers of refugees sink the lifeboat? Would the nation loose its freedoms with increased numbers? Would global demands of other nations swamp the U. S.? Was Professor Halfaaz right?

She knew too-well from personal experience the charming qualities of River City — quiet, fresh air, ease of movement, lack of stressful living — were being eroded daily by those bringing in more businesses and those bringing in more refugees and then complaining there wasn't enough housing for the poor. Would New York's noise, air pollution, high crime rate and tensions become River City's future with the flood of more people?

And what could she do about it? Did she have any responsibility? All the marches for peace seemed so silly, so shallow, so trivial and misdirected a response.

What made America great and special? Was there an

objective answer to the question? Or was it all relative and everyone could find and live comfortably in his own answer?

What was truth? Did it matter? Were there any absolute truths?

She sat back and waited for her intuition to speak to her.

And all that came was the voice of her Grandmother: Millie you have sinned. Say your prayers and ask for God's forgiveness. Don't worry about the world's problems. The world is passing. The salvation of your soul is all that matters.

And what did her intuition and rational self have to respond to Grandmother? She shut her eyes and waited for answers.

All Millie wanted was peace.

* * *

EPILOGUE

Sunlight was peeping through the windows of the Dixie Lounge. Morning traffic was getting the best of the remains of the snowstorm, which amazingly had left little on the ground.

Before I could gather my wits, McAdam had retrieved his socks and shoes from the fake fireplace, put them on, thanked me for dinner, and was on his way out the door.

"Wait a minute!" I stood up with one sock on. "I've got questions!"

"Sorry, son. No time. Have clients to meet. Places to go, people to see." He combed his hair with his fingers and straightened his tie.

"You said something about at the heart of the story was government secrets and the fate of nations. . ."

"No," he corrected, "I said at the heart was darkness or government secrets and the fate of nations. You did get the moral dilemma part?"

"Yes, of course. So you're saying there was no governments secrets, no fate of nations...?"

"Maybe there was; maybe there wasn't. I'll give you a clue: Look to Render and the box he was carrying." He tapped an index finger on his nose and was out the door.

I ran after him, with one sock on, forgetting my shoes and other sock were hanging by the fake fireplace. "What was in the box Render was carrying?!" I cried.

He gave me an indignant look. "You don't expect me to reveal government secrets, do you?!" He turned and as quick as a rabbit, he disappeared around the corner.

My eyes were squinting from the sunlight and my feet told me to go back and get my shoes and the other sock.

I would get no more out of McAdam. From that day forward, he would deny even having told me anything about the Istanbul CLE.

The morning he walked out of the Dixie Lounge, I had a sock and shoes to put on, a hotel bill to pay and a plane to catch. Clients of my own were waiting in another city. Like a leaf in a stream, I was moved on from one immediate concern to the next. A series of immediate concerns that were my life.

In the years that followed, in idle moments, I often pondered the Istanbul CLE, whether any of it was true and whether Millie Sharp existed. Perhaps, one of the reasons I moved to River City, was to find out how much of the Istanbul CLE story was true.

I tracked down the attorneys McAdam had talked about. They laughed and denied they had ever been to Istanbul. One said, "What is McAdam smoking these days?!" Another said, "I think he's given you a taradiddle."

When I found Art Chalmers alive and well, I was convinced everything McAdam told me was indeed a taradiddle or a piscatorial prevarication.

But my mind would not let the matter drop. Everyone's universal denial made me suspicious. And so something drives me to continue the search. Like McAdam, himself, I search for the truth, and wonder: Who is the real Millie Sharp? The lady as beautiful as Greto Garbo and as smart as Pericles' mistress.

Maybe I can get one of the attorneys to talk. I've invited two of them to dinner this evening. I'm confident with the right drinks and cigars I'll get some answers!

FINI

Some Comments on ISTANBUL!

"Tom Eagan's a little bit quirky,
And his novels are often quite murky;
   But his latest, "'Stanbool,"
   Shows that Tom is no fool,
As a playwright he sure knows his Turkey!

Set in the mysterious East,
Descending into the belly of the beast;
   With Byzantine twists,
   In the Dardanelles' mists,
The book is a literary feast.

Tom tells of a group of attorneys,
And of their fantastical journeys;
   "'Stanbool" has no equal,
   (Unless there's a sequel,
And attorneys their journeys returnies.)"

           — Thomas A. McAdam, III
           Moot Point, Kentucky

"ISTANBUL!, a novella. Tom Eagan is at it again, poking sleighty fun at our foibles, yours and mine, our pretensions. No matter where — the venerable Hall Of Justice or New Albany, Indiana or the swarthiest Turkey this side of a Greek polemic — Eagan (who obviously has never been snowed) portrays what we are and what we profess to stand for. Bravo."
    — Gerald McDaniel, author of *Aindreas: The Messenger,*
      The Scribe, and (work in progress) *Night Sweats and*
         Graffiti

"I read the book cover to cover the day I got it. Well worth the reading!"
         — Tom Schwietz, Attorney

"A rollicking saga of the Old Near East."
— Maureen Sullivan, Curator, Alfred Frank
Memorial Archives

"I didn't have sex with that woman!"
— David O'Brien, Esq.

"Eagan has done it again; ISTANBUL! wisks a dozen of the Hall's characters out of their legal environment and plunges them into an unknown land of mystery and intrigue. ISTANBUL! becomes Eagan's best read todate with enough twists and turns to make any lawyer soil his briefs. I can't wait for the Times New Roman version!"
— Larry Simon
Scholar in Residence

"ISTANBUL! — #@!!##@#!! Even in novels I get bit parts!"
— R. J. Atkinson
Actor, Bit Player, New York City

"I just got off the roller coaster called ISTANBUL!, and my legs are still wobbly. The cars bump along slowly at first as the characters are introduced, but when the plot begins to take off it spins and whirls and plummets and loops until the very end, leaving the reader stunned and breathless. What an exotic adventure!"
— Mary Krause, actress

"I never understand Eagan's books."
— Don Heavrin

"The book doesn't even touch the surface of Turkey. Why does the author leave out stuff?"
— Martin Kute, Attorney

"This book will change your life and make America stronger! It's called **ISTANBUL!**"
— Col. James Daniel Peppercorne

"Interesting. If you read between the lines, you'll find there are no words there."
— J. Andrew White, Esq.

"The best novel I never read!"
— Matt Stein, trial lawyer

"Not since Billy Hayes and his nemesis Rifke in 'Midnight Express' have I found a story with Turkish roots so suspenseful!!"
— Stan Chauvin, Notary Public at Large and Constitutional law scholar

"What can be said of Eagan or 'the Eagan,' as his contemporaries refer to him? Perhaps only comparison to Hollywood characters, bigger than life, can accomplish what words alone cannot. He possesses the worldly and scientific knowledge (and fashion sense) of Dr. Frankerfurter of the Rocky Horror Picture Show. The gentle kindness of Frank Booth of Blue Velvet, who just wants to take his neighbors for a joy ride. Or, perhaps that paradigm of military patriotism as portrayed by Robert Duvall in Apocalypse Now who proclaims, 'I love the smell of napalm in the morning. . . it smells like. . . victory. . . ' As any reader of his knows, Eagan is the smell of napalm in the morning."
— Gregory Ward Butrum, Attorney

". . . ?!!"
— Robert Render

NEXT IN THE TALES OF THE HALL SERIES

THE SKULL (Number 5 in Tales of the Hall)

The quixotic Bob Schaad, an attorney with boundless energy for defending the poor, ventures forth from the great Hall, into a rural county of quiet nights and lush vegetation to defend an old client facing a life in the penitentiary.

Schaad's old client is charged with beating up his daughter's high school biology teacher. There are plenty of witnesses to the beating. It looks like a lost cause till Schaad conceives of a defense that the assault on the biology teacher was justified! It was educational malpractice on the biology teacher's part not to allow a presentation of Intelligent Design in a high school biology class.

Intelligent Design is the view of a growing number of scientists that biological structures display design. If Intelligent Design is valid science, the implication is obvious: There is a Creator. Intelligent Design calls into question the validity of Darwinism which holds that all things biological have come about by "natural" causes (accident) and the "laws" of physics. No Creator need apply; discussion of a Creator is unscientific. Darwinism has held a vice grip on philosophical, scientific, sociological *and legal* thinking for a century. Marx, Freud and Hitler all found justification in Darwinism, as do secularists today.

The young prosecutor is speechless. The old judge, however, is going to allow Schaad to present his defense. The Powers That Be in the county of quiet nights and lush vegetation are not happy. They call upon the services of one of the nation's most brilliant trial attorneys, Don Heavrin, to assist the young prosecutor.

THE SKULL gives the reader a front row seat as two great legal minds battle over exactly what the sacred cow of the modern age (Science) is telling us.

Available December 2005.

Some other works of Tom Eagan
available from Aran Press

Plays

And I Was King?
Current Affairs
Feast of the Dancing Monkey
Love in New Albany
Murder For One
Puppy Love
Stay Out of the South
Temps
Thank You For Shopping at Bandweights
Things Made of Brass
Till We Love
The Unsuccessful Kroitzer
When A Girl Says "Yes"

Novellas

Fire Dancers of Bali
By Love Repossessed
Rumors of Justice
Joan of Doreme

Miscellaneous

Autumn Sonnets
Sayings of the Seer